UNDAUNTED

Praise for the book

In this anthology, Chidambaram is at his incisive best as he debunks the Modi bluff, bluster and braggadocio. He is eminently qualified to do so as he has had a long and distinguished innings in public life and has been Union Minister for both Finance and Home. His writings have scholarly archival value as well.

Jairam Ramesh,
Member of Parliament and Former Union Minister

Chidambaram brings to bear a wealth of experience, mastery of the subject matter, a sharp mind and engaging writing style to comment on contemporary economic and political issues. You may not agree with him, but you cannot ignore him.

Duvvuri Subbarao,
Former Governor, Reserve Bank of India

Chidambaram's essays cover some of India's disadvantages, which have accumulated over the years, due to socio-economic realities. Besides being an active politician, he is very articulate and erudite in sociology, law and economics.

Ashok Ganguly,
Former Member of Parliament

UNDAUNTED
SAVING THE IDEA OF INDIA

P. CHIDAMBARAM

Published by
Rupa Publications India Pvt. Ltd 2019
7/16, Ansari Road, Daryaganj
New Delhi 110002

Sales Centres:

Allahabad Bengaluru Chennai
Hyderabad Jaipur Kathmandu
Kolkata Mumbai

Copyright © P. Chidambaram 2019

Reprinted from *The Indian* EXPRESS

The views and opinions expressed in this book are the author's own and the facts are as reported by him which have been verified to the extent possible, and the publishers are not in any way liable for the same.

All rights reserved.
No part of this publication may be reproduced, transmitted, or stored in a retrieval system, in any form or by any means, electronic, mechanical, photocopying, recording or otherwise, without the prior permission of the publisher.

ISBN: 978-93-5333-373-7

First impression 2019

10 9 8 7 6 5 4 3 2 1

The moral right of the author has been asserted.

Printed in Inida by Gopsons Papers Ltd.

This book is sold subject to the condition that it shall not, by way of trade or otherwise, be lent, resold, hired out, or otherwise circulated, without the publisher's prior consent, in any form of binding or cover other than that in which it is published.

CONTENTS

FOREWORD BY M. HAMID ANSARI   ix
INTRODUCTION   xiii

GOVERNANCE

MINIMUM GOVERNMENT, MAXIMUM DAMAGE	3
SOUTHERN FLAMES MAY SCALD THE NATION	7
WILL GOVERNMENT WRECK FEDERALISM?	11
SEARCHING FOR SHANGRI-LA	15
BJP RENDERS AID AND ADVICE TO LIEUTENANT GOVERNOR!	19
FRANCE WINS HONOURS, CROATIA WINS HEARTS	23
FIRST ANARCHY, NOW AUTARKY	27
EMULATE, DO NOT ENVY	31
SHE WANTED REASONS, HERE ARE TEN	35
POWER LIES IN NON-USE	38
THE DAY OF RECKONING	41
ANOTHER INSTITUTION IS FALLING	45
THE FAMILIAR SOUND OF THE DRUMS	49
RAFALE JUDGMENT AND THE UNAVOIDABLE OPTION	52
THE YEAR ENDS ON A SOMBRE NOTE	56

ECONOMY

TRUTH, POST-TRUTH AND AGAIN THE TRUTH	63
THE 70 LAKH BOAST	67
WHAT HAPPENED TO INDRADHANUSH?	71
THE ONE-TRICK PONY IN DELHI	75
WHO IS MINDING THE STORE?	79
GOVERNMENTS HIDE, PEOPLE SEEK	83
CALCULATE PRICE OF A TRADE WAR	87

DEBATE, QUESTIONS, BUT NO ANSWERS	91
BLACK TO WHITE MAGIC	95
A BIG ASK IN ELECTION YEAR	99
FIVE STEPS TO NIRVANA	102
THINGS FALL APART; THE CENTRE CANNOT HOLD	106

BUDGET

COURAGE FAILS, RHETORIC REMAINS	113
GOOD DOCTOR, BAD PATIENT	116
MORE VOICES AGAINST BUDGET PROVISIONS	120
THE HOLE IN THE BUDGET	124

POLITICS

A MESSAGE LOUD AND CLEAR	131
CHANGE BEGINS WITH WORDS AND IDEAS	135
STATE ELECTION, NATION-WIDE EFFECT	139
WHO WILL SAVE THE CONSTITUTION?	142
MR A.B. VAJPAYEE, RIP	145
WILL CONSTITUTIONAL VALUES SURVIVE ELECTIONS?	148
A HUNDRED-DAY JOURNEY	151

JAMMU AND KASHMIR

REVISITING JAMMU AND KASHMIR	157
INDIA IS FAILING THE TEST ON JAMMU AND KASHMIR	161
THE REMAINS OF THE DAY	165
IN JAMMU AND KASHMIR, THE ROAD TO DISASTER	169

THE SOCIAL CHALLENGE

CELEBRATING GODS, NEGLECTING CHILDREN—2	175
FOR HEALTHCARE, BUDGET GIFTS A *JUMLA*	179
THE REPUBLIC OF IMPUNITY	183
SECOND-CLASS CITIZENS?	186
SU-RAJ (GOOD GOVERNANCE) AND MS SWARAJ	189
JOBS—THE MAKE OR BREAK ISSUE	192

GOOD AADHAAR, BAD AADHAAR	195
WE HAVE FAILED OUR CHILDREN	199
THOSE WHO ARE LEFT BEHIND	202

FOREIGN POLICY
ONE-MAN BAND CANNOT MAKE MUSIC	209
ENGAGING WITH MR IMRAN KHAN	213
EPILOGUE	217
ABBREVIATIONS	219

FOREWORD

Shri Chidambaram is nothing if not consistent, focused and prolific. For four years now his weekly commentaries have made available to interested readers facts and analysis of facts that remain undisputed. Together, they constitute a compendium on the state of the nation. The present volume is timely because in the coming months the citizens of this polity would exercise one of the most fundamental of their democratic rights, the franchise, to pronounce upon the performance of the government.

In ages gone by, a powerful advocate of democracy had opined that citizens 'are fair judges' of policy. This remains the standard by which to assess the pronouncements *and* performance of public leaders, whether they are statesmen or demagogues. This scrutiny has to go beyond the surface and explore the interstices and processes that led to individual acts of decision-making. It has to identify the gap between profession and practice and share it with the citizen body. Free societies over the world welcome it while those who view freedom differently deprecate it.

In times when criticism of state action is frowned upon, our author is undaunted. He has in these columns examined most aspects of our polity. An international journal of repute has this month enquired if India is faltering in its commitment to liberal, pluralistic, democratic order? The concern is serious and the quest for an answer would seem to lie firstly in our adherence to proclaimed principles and secondly to the efficacy of institutions.

What then is the score card?

There is no ambiguity about principles. These are inscribed in the Preamble and text of the Constitution—Justice, Liberty, Equality and Fraternity. So every action violating these principles or condoning their violation is a contravention and many instances of both are cited in these essays. The same holds for the efficacy of institutions. These are instruments of governance. Are they being used or misused? While a decline has been in progress for some time, it has been aggravated in recent years. Instances are many. If the Budget is passed without scrutiny and debate by the Parliament; and if important pieces of legislation are endorsed without reference to standing committees or select committees, then it is evident that the Parliament as the designated legislative institution is not doing its duty and the government of the day is failing in its primary duty.

The same holds for several other institutions. Some have imploded, others have faltered on their essential functions. Still others have succumbed to backdoor control. Together they raise doubts in the public mind and undermine the confidence essential in a normal, open, system.

The author highlights the resulting situation and draws attention to 'the belief in impunity that seems to have infected every public functionary' as a result of which 'every value of the Constitution is under attack—freedom, equality, liberalism, secularism, privacy, scientific temper, etc.' He concludes that 'there is a clear and present danger that the Constitution of India will be replaced by a document that will be inspired by an ideology called *Hindutva*.' This ideological deviation, conscious and unabashedly public, undermines the core values of the Constitution, differentiates between citizens on grounds of faith, seeks to impose a single cultural denominator to homogenize a plural society, and undermines secularism and the principle of fraternity.

The four essays on the situation in Jammu and Kashmir (J&K) make disturbing reading. From all available accounts, the 'muscular, militaristic policy' has caused alienation particularly among the youth. The late Shri Vajpayee had suggested a solution within the ambit of humanity (*insaniyat ke daere main*). We seem to have opted instead for inhumanity, forgetting the old dictum—might does not make right.

The essay on 'Searching for Shangrila' on India's place in the world should be read along with the 'Chilling Facts' on 'Those Who Are Left Behind.' This is perhaps the best commentary on the record of governance; this is how the world beyond our borders sees us.

Shri Chidambaram has done a public service by collecting these essays in this volume.

M. Hamid Ansari
14 January 2019

INTRODUCTION

When I resumed my column *Across the Aisle* in January 2015, I decided to write mainly on economic and social issues but also, I thought, occasionally on politics and foreign policy. I was apprehensive if I would be able to turn out an essay every Friday for publication on the following Sunday. I was also afraid that I would run out of subjects; that I will miss the deadline on many weeks; and that I may, in a short time, find the whole exercise burdensome and a chore.

If none of the above happened, I must thank Mr Narendra Modi and his government.

Although, initially, seven days in a week seemed too few, I found that the adrenalin would start flowing on Wednesday and, however busy I was, I would find the time to turn out a draft by Thursday. I was never at a loss for a subject. If economics did not throw up an issue, I turned to politics which provided an abundant supply of issues. And far from finding the exercise a chore, it turned out that the last four years have been the most challenging and eventful that I have spent as an Opposition politician.

My columns were less about what was happening *in* India and more about what was happening *to* India. And that is the conversation that I wish to have with you in this brief introduction to this book, or rather, this collection of columns written in 2018. They appeared in *The Indian Express* and other newspapers in English and nine other languages. Like many of you, I feel deeply and strongly about the developments of the last four years and I shall tell you, briefly, what is happening *to* India.

The Economy, Society

Top of the list is, of course, the economy. An economy that had recovered from the damage caused by the international financial crisis of 2008 (the 'Great Recession') and that was cruising at a growth rate of 7.5 per cent (old series, old methodology) has been derailed. Every one who brought sensible ideas to the table to turn the economy around has left the government in disgust or despair. Because there are no jobs; there is no relief to farmers; credit is scarce to micro, small and medium industries; manufacturing, construction and exports are languishing; more projects are stalled; and more companies are in insolvency, the government is manufacturing statistics and asking people to eat statistics.

As worrying as the damage done to the economy, is the damage done to the society. An old civilization that has accommodated many religions, cultures, languages, communities and castes, and has tried during the last 71 years to become a modern nation, is so polarized and divided today that there is real cause to worry about its survival. Political power is a trust; what is given can be taken away. No trustee, however strong in the courage of his convictions, can use the power to eliminate all opposition to him and aspire to perpetuate himself and his party in power. Atal Bihari Vajpayee, a life-long RSS *swayamsevak* understood the fundamental rules of a democracy and gracefully gave up power after 13 days, again after 13 months, and once again after 5 years. His example has been forgotten—and perhaps rubbished in private—by the *swayamsevaks* in power today. That will explain the brazen attempt to rewrite the rules of a parliamentary democracy and to erect, on the ruins of a parliamentary democracy, a theocratic, majoritarian and authoritarian State.

Constitutional Values

An economy derailed can be put back on the rails after enduring some pain and suffering. A society divided can be healed and united by selfless leaders taking the message of fraternity across the country as well as by average, decent men and women working in their own neighbourhoods. There is, however, one thing that cannot be fixed if it is broken, and that is the Constitution of India and the Constitutional values embodied in that document. Presently, every value of the Constitution is under attack—freedom, equality, liberalism, secularism, privacy, scientific temper, etc. There is a clear and present danger that the Constitution of India will be replaced by a document that will be inspired by an ideology called *Hindutva*. That will be the end of the 'idea of India' given to us by the founding fathers; and to restore that idea will require nothing less than another freedom struggle and another Mahatma.

I have no hesitation in saying that, today, fear rules India. Every individual lives in fear—fear of the neighbour, fear of self-styled moral brigades, fear of the law applied with an evil mind and unequal hand and, above all, fear of the snooping Indian State. Fear and freedom cannot go together. Fear drives freedom away. If we must reclaim our freedom we must drive fear away. It is not an easy task, but we cannot give up. Average citizens have summoned the courage to push back against a State in by-elections and elections to State legislatures; however, the task is unfinished, and it must be accomplished in the next hundred days. We have to carry on, undaunted, until we complete the task.

The Mind Is without Fear

Given the circumstances, it was easy to choose the title of this book. The essays in this collection chronicle the events that happened in 2018. They have been grouped, subject-wise, into sections and arranged chronologically within each section. I have no doubt that if the reader reads all the essays in one section, she will get a clear understanding of the course of events that affected the country—for better or worse—during 2018.

My greatest satisfaction has been that though I write in English I am read in Hindi, Punjabi, Marathi, Gujarati, Malayalam, Kannada, Telugu, Bengali and Urdu. The column is available online, it is also tweeted, and so, I believe, there are many thousands of readers of the column. It is brought out in the form of a book so that those who missed reading the column every week can have an opportunity to do so. The book will also serve as a contemporary record of the most important events of the year.

I urge you to read all the essays, section-wise, but if you want to get into my mind and understand my motivation to write a weekly column over four years—a total of 211 columns—you could start with 'The Republic of Impunity' (page 183). Although the BJP considers all Opposition politicians as enemies who have to be exterminated, I do not regard the BJP as an enemy. To me, it is a political party that is at the extreme right of Indian politics and it is for the people of India to accept or reject the party. If you want to know about my attitude to the BJP, please read the essays on 'Ms Sushma Swaraj' (page 189) and 'Mr A.B. Vajpayee' (page 145). If you wish to dissect my views on the economy, there are many essays and you may like to begin with 'Debate, Questions, but no Answers' (page 91). And, finally, if you want to find out the real person inside me, I suggest you start with 'Those Who Are Left Behind' (page 202) and read all the essays in that section.

Have I won a lot of readers? Yes. Have I influenced the thinking of many of them? Possible. Have I converted anyone to my point of view? I do not know. Have I made the central government mend its policies and methods? NO, in capital letters, and I have no illusion that I or anyone else can influence the ways of the present government. Every distinguished scholar who offered or came to work with this government was banished—and that tells the story.

As a free citizen, I can—and must—shed fear, oppose tyranny, speak freely, write boldly and carry on undaunted by the power of the State. I hope you too will do that. It is within your power and it is what you owe to the country.

P. Chidambaram

GOVERNANCE

I am not surprised that the most number of essays that I wrote in 2018 concerned 'governance'. After making a mess of the economy, the central government began to interfere with institutions like the Reserve Bank of India (RBI) and the Finance Commission. It turned the Constitution on its head and argued that the lieutenant governor of Delhi, and not the elected government, held the real power—and was snubbed by the Supreme Court. The true intentions of the BJP became clear as the months went by. Naturally, I wrote many essays on the dangers that I foresaw if the BJP's model of governance were allowed to go unchallenged.

MINIMUM GOVERNMENT, MAXIMUM DAMAGE

4 March 2018

The most misused cliche about governance is 'That country is governed best which is governed least'. The cliche has depreciated so much that its value, in contemporary governance, is close to zero.

There are several models of governance. In a unitary or federal, but statist economy, the model is one of total control by the central government (e.g. North Korea) or with some control shared with the appointed provincial governments (e.g. the erstwhile Soviet Union). China introduced a *sui generis* model: it kept near total control with the central government but allowed private players to make business decisions. China called it 'Socialism with Chinese characteristics'.

Open liberal economies—whether under a unitary or a federal Constitution—followed a different path. The starting point was *laissez faire*. In the early years of modern capitalism, it was believed that anything goes under *laissez faire*. The so-called robber barons of the United States enriched themselves but they also created wealth and jobs. The system produced enormous inequalities. It was also vulnerable to gross failures, violent trade union action and other excesses.

Control vs Regulation

Obviously, *laissez faire*, as prevalent, could not continue and the State could not remain a silent spectator. The era of regulation began.

Regulation is not control. Countries with open, liberal and market economies struggled to discover the difference between control and regulation. It took them years to put in place appropriate regulatory mechanisms—not amounting to control—and appoint qualified regulators. On the other hand, countries that started with control and are now liberalizing—like India—are still struggling to discover the difference, and often end up with either the government exercising remote control or regulators morphing into controllers.

This essay is concerned with one kind of erosion of liberal democratic governance—the Executive Government insidiously acquiring control by diminishing or debilitating other organs of the State and other regulators established by law. The National Democratic Alliance (NDA) government seems to have perfected the craft.

Gaping Holes in the System

Look at the Table:

Organization/Statutory Authority	Sanctioned Strength	Vacancies
Supreme Court of India	31	7
Judges, High Courts	1,079	403
Chief Justices, High Courts	24	9
Deputy Governors, RBI	4	1
SEBI (Members)	9	2
Securities Appellate Tribunal	3	1
National Green Tribunal	11	6
Income Tax Appellate Tribunal	126	34
Central Administrative Tribunal	66	24
Central Information Commission Commissioners Other Staff	11 160	4 79

Central Vigilance Commission		
Commissioners	3	1
Other Staff	296	53
IPS cadre	4,843	938
CBI	7,274	1,656
Central Universities		
Vice-Chancellors	41	3
Teaching Posts	17,106	5,997

Can a country with a population of 132 crore have in its higher judiciary (high courts and the Supreme Court) only 1,110 posts of judges, of which 410 are vacant? The gainer is the largest litigant (the central government) whose illegal actions, and inactions, are the subject matter of thousands of cases that remain pending for years.

The same can be said about the other authorities and bodies. The key post of deputy governor, RBI, in charge of the Department of Banking Supervision, has remained vacant since 31 July 2017—yet we bemoan the failure of supervision over the Punjab National Bank (PNB) and other banks! Key regulators and tribunals are running on two or three wheels.

The Hidden Agenda

The purpose of this essay is to ask 'Is this the minimum government that was promised by the Bharatiya Janata Party (BJP) in the run-up to the parliamentary elections in 2014?' The more important follow-up questions are 'Who benefits by keeping posts vacant in crucial regulators and authorities?' and 'Who benefits from fewer Right to Information (RTI) disclosures and fewer tax case judgments?' The answers are obvious.

We must understand the true nature of the Rashtriya Swayamsevak Sangh (RSS) and its offspring, the BJP. The RSS is an authoritarian organization: one purpose, one thought, one credo and one leader. When it captures the government through its political arm, it tries to impose on the people its pet theories of one history, one culture, one language ('Hindi is our national language'), one religion ('All those who live in Hindustan are Hindus'), one civil code and one election.

Democracy in its true sense—liberal, multiple voices and thoughts, and checks and balances—is antithetical to the RSS/BJP way of governance. If other institutions of a democracy are weakened, it gives greater power, in the real and practical sense, to the Executive. Hence, the deliberate effort to keep other institutions weak and debilitated. And even when appointments are made, they are totally centralized in the Prime Minister's Office and done after what is widely known in Delhi—profiling. The latest victim of profiling is Justice K.M. Joseph.

Minimum government is intended to acquire maximum control, liberal democracy be damned.

SOUTHERN FLAMES MAY SCALD THE NATION

8 April 2018

The Constitution of India obliges the President (i.e. the central government) to appoint, every five years, a Finance Commission (Article 280). Its foremost duty is 'to make recommendations to the President as to the distribution between the Union and the States of the net proceeds of taxes which are to be...divided between them... and the allocation between the States of the respective shares of such proceeds'.

There are other duties, but they are not germane to the controversy dealt with in this essay.

On the first part of the duty mentioned above, the states are together: they demand a greater share of the taxes from every Finance Commission (FC). As per the last FC (the Fourteenth), the states' share was fixed at 42 per cent.

It is on the second part mentioned above—allocation between the states of the respective shares—that a controversy has erupted. Every state wants a larger share of the pie, but the total cannot exceed 100 per cent (of the 42 per cent). It is also not possible to freeze the respective shares of the states because the objective conditions for allocation of the respective shares may, and would, have changed in five years. If a state's share is reduced even by a fraction, the state is unhappy. Every FC has an unenviable task, but none more than the Fifteenth FC that was constituted in November 2017.

Questionable Departure

The reason lies in the Terms of Reference (ToR) of the Fifteenth FC. The main ToR remain on the usual lines, but there are two significant departures from the past.

Firstly, the Fifteenth FC has been asked to consider certain performance-based incentives, including:

- Efforts and progress made in moving towards replacement rate of population growth;
- Implementation of schemes of the Government of India;
- Control in incurring expenditure on populist measures.

Secondly, the FC shall use population data from the 2011 Census and not the 1971 Census that was used hitherto. Both changes are big changes that have serious implications for Centre-states relations. Structurally, the Constitution gives more powers of taxation to the Centre and more responsibilities of expenditure to the states.

Hence the need for a fair system of sharing the Centre's net tax revenues. A state legislature has as much power over the state's budget as Parliament has over the Union Budget. The FC is not a mechanism to impose the will—or the schemes—of the central government on the states. Constitutionally, a state is entitled to say 'give me my fair share of taxes and leave me alone to act according to the decisions of my state legislature'.

Punishing Performance

The second change is highly controversial. Hitherto, the population data was taken from the 1971 Census. The 'freeze' was agreed upon to protect the states that had done well in stabilizing their population. The Fourteenth FC made a small shift: it reduced the weightage to the 1971 Census data from 25 to 17.5 per cent and introduced a weightage of 10 per cent to the 2011 Census data. Directing the Fifteenth FC to discard the 1971 Census data and take into account only the 2011 Census data, is a clear punishment for states that had performed splendidly between 1971 and 2011 in stabilizing their population.

The argument that poorer states with less fiscal capacity, less revenues, historical disadvantages and poorer development outcomes deserve more support is a sound argument. It was acknowledged by the Fourteenth FC when it raised the weightage given to 'fiscal capacity' from 47.5 to 50 per cent—the highest for any factor. However, shifting the population data from the 1971 Census to the 2011 Census cannot be justified: in fact, it is a perverse incentive to states that had neglected to stabilize their population.

Better-governed and better-performing states have already lost crucial fractions in their shares (see Table):

State	Percentage Share as Determined by the				
	10th FC	11th FC	12th FC	13th FC	14th FC
Andhra Pradesh*	8.465	7.701	7.356	6.937	6.742
Karnataka	5.339	4.930	4.459	4.328	4.713
Kerala	3.875	3.057	3.665	2.341	2.500
Tamil Nadu	6.637	5.385	5.305	4.969	4.023
Total	24.316	21.073	19.785	18.575	17.978

*undivided

Douse the Fire Now

The southern states have lost 6.338 per cent on account of better governance and better outcomes, but they were at least protected against the consequences of a fall in their share of India's population. According to the 1971 Census, their population was 24.7 per cent of the total population; according to the 2011 Census data it had fallen to 20.7 per cent. If all other factors are kept constant, the mandate to the Fifteenth FC to consider the population according to the 2011 Census will further reduce the shares of the southern states.

Post-1991, every state could take advantage of a more open

economy, less control and state-specific strategies. States that were once regarded as having low potential now claim to have achieved high growth rates. We may empathize with the states that are relatively poorer, but we cannot ignore the rights and aspirations of the better-performing states.

The central government has lit a fire. It should be doused before the southern flames scorch the federation.

WILL GOVERNMENT WRECK FEDERALISM?

15 April 2018

As I had feared last week, the fire that was lit by the ToR of the Fifteenth Finance Commission (FC) has spread. No effort has been made to douse the fire. Under Article 280, it is the constitutional right of the states, *together*, to get the states' share of taxes; it is also the constitutional right of *each state* to get its fair share out of the total states' share. The FC is no one's servant; its master is the Constitution alone. The current share of the states (as per the Fourteenth FC) is 42 per cent. No one expects that number will be reduced by the Fifteenth FC.

Another duty is cast upon the FC, by Article 280(3)(b), to recommend 'the principles which should govern the grants-in-aid of the revenues of the states out of the Consolidated Fund of India.' This provision has to be read with Article 275, which enables Parliament to provide each year 'grants-in-aid of the revenues' of such states that are in need of assistance. So, the sequence is, the Constitution imposes a duty, the FC will recommend the principles, and Parliament will provide the grants to the states.

Questionable Terms

In the ToR of the Fifteenth FC, paragraphs 2, 3, 4 and 5 are crucial. Para 2 contains an unusual mix of 'shall' and 'may'. The 'may' part is worrying and reads, 'The Commission may also examine whether revenue deficit grants be provided at all.' Para 3 contains matters that the FC shall have regard to. Much of it is along the usual lines, but sub-para (iv) injects a political element: 'the continuing imperative of the national development programme including New India–2022.'

Para 4 contains matters that the FC may consider. This is where more political elements have been introduced, such as:

- Efforts and progress made in moving towards replacement rate of population growth;
- Progress made...in promoting savings by adoption of Direct Benefit Transfers (DBTs)...promoting digital economy;
- Control or lack of it in incurring expenditure on populist measures.

Para 5 is fundamentally biased. It mandates that 'the Commission shall use the population data of 2011 while making its recommendations'.

The States Protest

States that have carefully analysed the implications of the ToR are up in arms. The first move was made by the southern states, at a meeting convened by Kerala. Of the five states and the UT of Puducherry, Tamil Nadu and Telangana were absent. My guess is that Tamil Nadu was absent because of fear of the BJP and Telangana was absent because of its ambivalence about the BJP.

I list below the questions that arise out of the ToR. The states should raise these questions before the central government and demand answers.

1. Can the central government ask the FC to examine whether revenue grants should be provided at all? Under Article 280(3)(b) it is the duty of the FC to recommend the principles in this behalf. Under Article 275 it is the right of Parliament to make a law providing those grants. How can the Executive (i.e. central government) attempt to thwart that process? It is unconstitutional.
2. What is New India–2022? As of now, it is a mere slogan of the prime minister. It is not part of any development programme

approved by a body like the National Development Council or Parliament. There will be an election in April-May 2019 long before the Fifteenth FC will submit its report by 30 October 2019. How can the FC be mandated to take into account a slogan of a political party?

3. Which are the states that will be benefited by considering 'the efforts and progress made in moving towards replacement rate of population growth'? Certainly not the states that have already achieved or gone below the replacement rate many years ago. They have achieved that target by spending more on health, education and family planning, but will now get less money to spend on the health and education needs of their people!

4. DBTs and Digital Economy are matters that will be constantly debated. Should foodgrain be provided to the poor or should cash-for-grain be transferred under the DBT? How far and how fast should 'digitisation' be rolled out in a state? These are questions concerning the political economy and are best addressed by elected governments and legislatures, not through recommendations of the FC.

5. What is a 'populist measure'? When Kamaraj introduced the mid-day meal scheme in schools in Tamil Nadu, it was criticised as populist; today it is a national programme.

State	Loss (₹Crore)
Andhra & Telangana	24,340
Tamil Nadu	22,497
Kerala	20,285
West Bengal	20,022
Odisha	18,545
Karnataka	8,373
Assam	5,136

6. What will be the cost to some states because of the mandate to discard the 1971 census data—agreed by consensus and

embodied in policy statements—and take into account the 2011 data? Mr V. Bhaskar (EPW, 10 March 2018) has calculated the loss to states, on this count alone, if the Fourteenth FC had taken into account the 2011 data. Under Fifteenth FC, the loss to these states will be more.

The fire will not be doused by specious arguments pitting 'populous and poorer states' against diligent and developed states. All states have poverty and developmental deficiencies. They should be addressed without bias and without wrecking federalism.

SEARCHING FOR SHANGRI-LA

17 June 2018

Shangri-La is believed to be a mystical, harmonious valley, an earthly paradise and a permanently happy land. If there is a Shangri-La, it is not likely to be in India, and that will be a big disappointment for all Indians who take pride in the history, culture, civilizational attributes and traditions of the country.

Prime Minister Narendra Modi's outreach to the world has attracted widespread attention. Recently, he made an impressive speech at the Shangri-La dialogue in Singapore. It was a well-crafted speech and there are several passages that deserve to be quoted and read.

Diversity at Home

Early in his speech, he said: 'Singapore also shows that when nations stand on the side of principles, not behind one power or the other, they earn the respect of the world and a voice in international affairs. And, when they embrace diversity at home, they seek an inclusive world outside.'

Diversity at home is embedded in the idea of India. It includes diversity of religion, language, personal law, culture, food, dress, etc. Yet, there are powerful groups that oppose or ridicule diversity and insist on uniformity. They claim that all those who inhabit Hindustan are Hindus. They attempt to re-write history and re-claim what they believe is theirs, and seek to impose a uniform personal law, uniform food habits, uniform dress codes and one language. The world's leaders hear the prime minister and applaud his appeal to embrace diversity; and then they read about happenings in Dadri, Uttar Pradesh (Mohammed Akhlaq); Alwar, Rajasthan (Pehlu Khan); Una, Gujarat (Dalit boys); and Bhima Koregaon, Maharashtra (Dalit gathering). They shake their heads in disbelief and are confused. And a few days ago, two Muslims were lynched on suspicion of being cattle-lifters (Dullu, district Godda, Jharkhand) and three Dalit boys were beaten and paraded naked for swimming in a well (Vakadi, district Jalgaon, Maharashtra). Whither diversity that we advocate to the world?

Flunked Export-Import Test

Speaking on economic relations, the prime minister said: 'Coming back to our region. India's growing engagement is accompanied by deeper economic and defence cooperation. We have more trade agreements in this part of the world than in any other.'

To what intent and purposes did we enter into numerous agreements with the countries of the region? Why has India's trade with the SAARC countries and the ASEAN countries stagnated? Total trade, in 2013–14 and 2017–18, with SAARC countries was approximately USD 20 billion and USD 26 billion respectively. As a proportion of India's total trade with all countries, the numbers were 2.6 per cent and 3.4 per cent. In the case of ASEAN countries, the numbers for the two years were approximately USD 74 billion (9.7 per cent) and USD 81 billion (10.5 per cent). There is nothing in the record of the last four years to boast that there has been significant improvement.

Talking about India's economic growth, the prime minister said: 'We will sustain growth of 7.5 to 8 per cent per year. As our economy grows, our global and regional integration will increase. A nation of over 800 million youth knows that their future will be secured not just by the scale of India's economy, but also by the depth of global engagement.'

That is absolutely correct, but the government seems to have little understanding of the link between exports, manufacturing and jobs. The true measure of India's 'global engagement' is trade, and the government has flunked that test. In four years, merchandise export growth has been negative (from USD 315 billion to USD 303 billion). Imports have grown marginally from USD 450 billion to USD 465 billion. No country has lifted its manufacturing sector without robust export growth. And no country has created non-farm jobs without boosting the manufacturing sector. It is the failure of manufacturing and exports that has led many to suspect the GDP growth numbers that are thrown about. In any event, even the GDP growth rate has slumped from 8.2 per cent in 2015–16 to 6.7 per cent in 2017–18.

Path of Wisdom

And then the prime minister uttered carefully chosen words in the context of the global economy, but those words could have described the Indian situation as well:

'And, the future looks less certain. For all our progress, we live on the edge of uncertainty, of unsettled questions and unresolved disputes; contests and claims; and clashing visions and competing models.'

The closing passages of the prime minister's speech and the peroration were worthy of the occasion:

'We are inheritors of Vedanta philosophy that believes in essential oneness of all, and celebrates unity in diversity. Truth is one, the learned speak of it in many ways. That is the foundation of our civilisational ethos—of pluralism, co-existence, openness and dialogue.

'But, there is also a path of wisdom. It summons us to a higher purpose: to rise above a narrow view of our interests and recognise that each of us can serve our interests better when we work together as equals in the larger good of all…'

How true and how appropriate those words will be if they are addressed to the Vishwa Hindu Parishad, the Bajrang Dal, the Ram Sena, the Hanuman Sena, the anti-Romeo squads, the Akhil Bharatiya Vidyarthi Parishad and the several ministers, parliamentarians and legislators who reject the 'path of wisdom'.

I urge the prime minister to deliver a Shangri-La type speech in India and on the reality of India.

BJP RENDERS AID AND ADVICE TO LIEUTENANT GOVERNOR!

15 July 2018

The irony of our times is that the ordinary becomes extraordinary.

In any parliamentary democracy, judges and lawyers, parliamentarians and legislators, and ministers and civil servants know where the true power lies. It lies with the elected representatives who, among themselves, will choose a prime minister or a chief minister. There is another appointed functionary, called governor or lieutenant governor, who may enjoy the prestige attached to the office but is obliged to act on the aid and advice of the council of ministers.

The phrase 'aid and advice' is the cornerstone of representative government. Wherever it occurs, the unmistakable conclusion is that the person who renders the aid and advice is the one who holds real power and the person who receives the aid and advice is only the titular head. The principle is so well established that anyone who pretends to hold the opposite view is exactly that—a pretender.

No Ambiguity at All

Article 239AA(4) of the Constitution of India (which is a special provision with respect to Delhi) lays down in unambiguous terms that 'There shall be a Council of Ministers…with the Chief Minister at the head to aid and advise the Lieutenant Governor in the exercise of his functions…'

Section 44(a) of the Government of National Capital Territory of Delhi Act, 1991, reinforces the legal position. It provides for the allocation of business (to ministers) 'with respect to which the Lieutenant Governor is required to act on the aid and advice of his Council of Ministers'.

Mr Najeeb Jung and Mr Anil Baijal were not novices. They belonged to the IAS and were seasoned administrators. Besides, Mr Jung was, for some years, the vice-chancellor of Jamia Millia Islamia. Mr Baijal had held several important posts in his career, including Union home secretary and had dealt with the Delhi government. Both knew exactly what they were doing as the lieutenant governor of Delhi, yet if they did act in a peculiar manner, it was not because of ignorance but because of subservience. They acted like the viceroys of the British Raj and, in the process, assaulted the fundamental tenets of a representative democracy.

Every Argument Rejected

Recently, the Supreme Court held that the Delhi government had legislative and executive power on all subjects except three—land, police and public order. The central government's and BJP's spokespersons may now say that the judgment of the Supreme Court did not lay down new law but only reiterated the old legal position. If that is correct, the logical conclusion is that the judgment of the High Court, Delhi (which was reversed by the Supreme Court), was wrong and bad in law. Ask the central government why it had stoutly defended the wrong judgment before the Supreme Court; I am certain the spokespersons and the blog writers will not condescend to answer!

Not one of the central government's main arguments found favour with the Court and they were comprehensively rejected:

- The government contended that 'the ultimate administration with respect to Delhi shall remain with the President acting through its administrator'—Rejected.

- The government contended that 'although Article 239AA confers on the Legislative Assembly of Delhi the power to legislate with respect to subject matters provided in List II and List III of the Seventh Schedule, yet the said power is limited by the very same Article'—Rejected.
- The government contended that 'it is the "Lieutenant Governor" and not the "Council of Ministers" who is responsible for the administration of the Union Territory'—Rejected.
- The government contended that 'the principle…wherever there is existence of legislative power there is co-extensive existence of executive power, is with respect to only the Union and the states and is not applicable to Union Territories'—Rejected.
- The government contended that 'the aid and advice rendered by the Council of Ministers is not binding upon the Lieutenant Governor'—Rejected.
- The government contended that 'the phrase "any matter" in Article 239AA(4) has to be interpreted to mean "every matter"'—Rejected.

Backdoor Control

Having lost in the swings, the ill-advised central government is trying to win in the roundabouts. It says that Services (meaning appointments, transfers and postings of civil servants in the Delhi government) will continue to be under the control of the lieutenant governor. The central government is spoiling for another fight with the Delhi government, and the first shots were fired by Mr Baijal when, post-judgment, he ordered transfers and postings of three senior officers. In my view, Mr Baijal was wrong and his wrong action proves that he is acting at the behest of the BJP-led central government.

Recent blogs have revealed that the inspiration behind the central government's submissions before the Supreme Court was, among others, Mr Arun Jaitley. Not reconciled to the unanimous judgment of the Constitution Bench, Mr Jaitley has once again set up another legal battle on the question of control of Services. In his blog he wrote, 'any presumption that the administration of the UT cadre of Services has been decided in favour of the Delhi Government would be wholly erroneous'. Is Mr Jaitley suggesting that the elected Delhi government may exercise executive powers but will have no control over the civil servants who will discharge the responsibilities?

The argument defies common sense. But there will be another judgment day.

FRANCE WINS HONOURS, CROATIA WINS HEARTS

22 July 2018

France beat Croatia 4-2 in the FIFA World Cup final and both countries emerged winners! All of France is deliriously happy, all of Croatia is proud and happy.

Everyone knows something about France. It was a colonial power, it is a nuclear power, it is among the five veto-holding members of the United Nations (UN) Security Council, it is a member of the European Union, NATO and G7, and it has Paris and the Eiffel Tower.

What do we know about Croatia? Very little. It was part of the erstwhile Yugoslavia, but Yugoslavia does not exist any more. It broke up into Croatia, Slovenia, Bosnia & Herzegovina, Montenegro, Serbia, Kosovo and Macedonia. Compared to France, Croatia is a minnow. France's land area is 10 times that of Croatia, its population is 15 times that of Croatia. Needless to say, France's GDP is 50 times the GDP of Croatia—USD 2,582 billion vs USD 55 billion. (Only a few days ago, the Government of India boasted that India's GDP had overtaken France's and we were the sixth largest economy in the world.)

Small vs Big

Can small countries match big countries? They cannot ever in land area or population or military power, but they can in other parameters that actually matter to the people. See how Croatia measures up in comparison with France (see Table).

	France	Croatia
Life expectancy at birth (in years)	82	78
Mortality rate, under 5 (per 1000 live births)	4	5
Fertility rate	2.0	1.4
Literacy rate (%)	99	99
Years of schooling	16.3	15.3
Gender Development Index	0.998	0.997
Gross Capital Formation*	23	21
Total exports*	30.9	51.3
Total imports*	32.0	49.1
Time required		
To start a business (days)	4	7
To get electricity (days)	71	65
Unemployment (% of total labour)	9.7	10.8

*(% of GDP)

Croatia's population is 41,25,700—about the same as Kanpur. Its income per capita is a commendable USD 13,295 which places it as a middle-income country. The country was ravaged by war during 1991–1995, but its people have lifted themselves up by the bootstraps. A look at the data will show that Croatia is highly globalised. It receives foreign direct investment that is 4 per cent of its GDP (or USD 500 per person). Croatians live long, are healthy, have few children, are secure within their borders, and not too worried about the fact that they are a small country that doesn't make the wrong headlines every day.

There are 195 countries in the world. 182 countries have a population of less than 100 million and nearly 107 countries have a population of less than 10 million. Small can be beautiful. Small countries can be modestly rich with their people enjoying a good quality of life—good enough to produce a world-class football team. On its way to the final, Croatia beat Nigeria, Argentina, Iceland, Denmark, Russia, England and drew with Switzerland. Other examples of small but prosperous countries are Iceland, Austria, Norway, Sweden and New Zealand.

Big countries (in size and/or population) too can be wealthy with their people enjoying a good quality of life. Examples are the United States, Canada and Australia—and now an aspirational China.

Invent Own Model

There is not one model that will apply to all countries. There is also not one model that can be applied to the constituents of a large, federal nation. We have to invent a model that will accommodate the peculiar characteristics of a large country like India, with numerous states, multiple races, many religions, thousands of languages, and different states at different stages of development and different rates of growth.

Such a model can be constructed in a federal country, provided it is based on some fundamental principles such as:

- Decentralization: Over the years, the central government has arrogated too many powers to itself leaving states with little autonomy and few resources. The first order of the day must be to respect the Constitutional distribution of legislative powers. List II of the Seventh Schedule is for the states; List III too should be with the states. Although titled Concurrent List, the time has come for the Centre to withdraw, as much as possible, from List III and allow the states to legislate on those subjects.
- Natural Resources: The central government should cede control over natural resources like coal, minerals, etc to the states in which they are located. Each state will then discover its comparative advantages and disadvantages and find ways to compete with other states. All states will benefit from such competition.
- Financial Resources: At present, states have been reduced to supplicants for money. This situation must be drastically

overhauled. The two taxes that will account for the bulk of the revenues are Income Tax (including Corporate Tax) and Goods and Services Tax (GST). Like in the case of GST, both the Centre and the states must have the power to levy Income Tax (including Corporate Tax) on incomes.

- Autonomy: On matters such as education, health care and health insurance, support prices, crop insurance, welfare measures, social security, etc, the states must have the authority and freedom to devise their own policies and design their own programmes. Many states will do a better job than the Centre is doing now.

That's transformational reform. And then we may dream of having a World Cup football team.

FIRST ANARCHY, NOW AUTARKY

12 August 2018

When I talk to young people below the age of 25 years, I find that one of the best ways to capture their attention—and regale them—is to tell them about 'booking a trunk call' or 'buying a scooter' in the good old days! Invariably, the listener will draw the following conclusions:

- That I was inventing the stories/experiences.
- That I am technologically challenged.
- That I am older than his/her grandfather who died 10 years ago.

The truth is that every word of the stories was true. A full 65 per cent of the population of India (that is under the age of 35 years) simply does not know what it was to live in a country where the governing economic principles were State control, primacy of the public sector, licencing, self-sufficiency, high tax rates and suspicion of the private sector (except in the case of agriculture).

When Autarky Ruled

Not that our leaders and policy makers were daft. Many of our leaders were highly educated, undoubtedly intelligent, and lived selfless, spartan lives. Our administrators were drawn from the cream of young men and women who had the privilege of a university education and a genuine desire to be useful citizens (besides job security). Yet, while progress was made, it was painfully slow with the

GDP growing, on average, at about 3.5 per cent, and per capita income at about 1.3 per cent a year for nearly 30 years after Independence.

That kind of economic regime has a name: autarky (meaning self-sufficiency as an economic system). China shed autarky in 1978, India in 1991.

Autarky will never be dead and buried six fathoms deep. It has a way of rearing its head from time to time, and that is what seems to be happening now under the BJP-led NDA government.

There is a vast difference between being market-friendly and business-friendly. Since its founding, the RSS has been an advocate of economic nationalism, *swadeshi* and self-reliance. Its trade union, Bharatiya Mazdoor Sangh, is opposed to foreign investment. One of its frontal organisations, the Swadeshi Jagran Manch, is unabashedly in favour of autarkic policies.

Back to the Past

In recent months, there is growing evidence that the BJP is reviving the instruments that were discarded long ago, as part of its narrative of hyper-nationalism. Let us look at some examples:

1. The 'market' exists irrespective of the State. Markets promote economic efficiency and freedom. Markets must be lightly regulated and the State should interfere in markets only in a few circumstances. Even countries that have embraced social democracy have found that the market economy is compatible with their economic philosophy (e.g. the Scandinavian countries).

   The BJP's position on the market economy is dubious. While claiming to be business-friendly, it has re-discovered the virtues of import substitution, tariff and non-tariff barriers, quantitative restrictions, price control and licences and permits. More instruments to control the economy have been deployed today than what were in place in 2014. Each decision can be traced to the lobbying of an 'interest group' that is usually a front for an individual business house.

2. Trade has been the driver of the unprecedented global growth witnessed since World War II. Millions of people have been pulled out of poverty. Small nations that were once considered unviable have flourished and have joined the ranks of high-income countries (e.g. Singapore, Taiwan). The principal instrument for pushing countries toward freer trade was the bilateral or multilateral trade agreement; and, since 1995, the World Trade Organization (WTO). The BJP-led government does not seem to believe in the usefulness of trade agreements and, by choice, India is no longer a powerful voice in the WTO. The most recent example is the appointment of a committee to review the utility of the proposed Regional Comprehensive Economic Partnership that will bind 10+6 countries to expand trade among themselves.

Price Will Be Heavy

3. The BJP-led government refuses to give up its obsession with levying retrospective taxes. The first thing it should have done in 2014 was to repeal the so-called Vodafone amendment to the Income Tax Act. On the contrary, not only is the tax demand on Vodafone being pursued, similar retrospective demands have been raised in respect of other transactions. Besides, the government tinkers with tax rates almost every month—e.g. Customs duties and GST rates (to undo the original sins).
4. Following in the footsteps of US President Trump, Mr Narendra Modi has signalled his support to protectionist policies. Protectionism will hurt consumers, curb demand and lead to misallocation of resources and wrong investment decisions. I am astonished that a task force has been constituted to identify ways and means to reduce imports! The draft rules on e-commerce are the latest example of muddled economic thinking. Rules on discounts that can be offered and inventory that can be held are glaring illustrations of the protectionist mindset.
5. Autarky can thrive only by empowerment of the bureaucracy, especially tax officials and investigation agencies. The BJP-

led government has done just that: conferring extraordinary powers (such as search, seizure and arrest) on more officials, and criminalisation of laws. For example, the Foreign Exchange Management Act was non-criminal; now it has a criminal law provision.

There was anarchy in policy-making—demonetisation and the deplorable implementation of the GST. Now, autarky has joined anarchy. I am afraid the country will pay a heavy price.

EMULATE, DO NOT ENVY

26 August 2018

A few days ago, a cheerleader for the BJP writing on the editorial page of a newspaper thanked Mr Arun Jaitley and me for engaging in a 'high quality debate on economic growth'. He reluctantly conceded that I had won the growth debate but charged that the Congress party had 'mismanaged the economy'. Thank you, but no thank you.

Mr Jaitley, on the previous day, had weighed in with the comment that 'UPA did no reform during its reign'. Firstly, the United Progressive Alliance (UPA) did not reign, it governed the country for 10 years and then bowed out of office. Secondly, if Mr Jaitley is right that no reforms were done during the UPA's 10 years, India must be the only country in world history that achieved double-digit growth (and average annual growth of over 8 per cent during 10 years) without implementing any reform!

UPA Vindicated

Some of you may have missed the development that triggered the debate. The development was the release of the back series data of GDP to be able to compare the growth rates of the past with the growth rates since 2012–13 when the base year was changed and a new methodology was adopted.

Here are the results (see Table):

	GDP at Factor Cost New Series Average Growth Rate	GDP at Market Prices New Series Average Growth Rate
NDA 1 (1999–2004)	5.69	5.68
UPA 1 (2004–2009)	8.87	8.36
UPA 2 (2009–2014)	7.39	7.68
NDA 2 (2014–2018)	n.a.	7.33

The conclusions are obvious: the 10-year period of the UPA recorded the highest decadal growth (8.02 per cent at market prices and 8.13 per cent at factor cost) since Independence. When the UPA demitted office, growth had recovered in 2013–14 to 6.39 per cent at market prices. The Modi government had inherited an economy that was on the upswing. Gross Fixed Capital Formation (GFCF) in 2013–14 was 31.3 per cent. Merchandise exports had scaled a new peak of USD 315 billion. Foreign Exchange reserves had reached a high of USD 304.2 billion.

Within four months of the NDA assuming office, the government got an unexpected bonanza through the collapse of crude oil and commodity prices. Both internal and external conditions were conducive for high growth, but the government squandered the opportunity. The first year was promising and the second year too started well. The first major blunder was demonetisation on 8 November 2016. This was followed by other blunders—flawed and hurried implementation of GST and tax terrorism. Between 2015–16 and 2017–18, the growth rate declined by 1.5 per cent—exactly what I had predicted immediately after demonetisation.

True Reforms

Reform is a word that has many meanings. It is usually associated with economic reforms, but there are reforms outside the economy that are as important as economic reforms and, in their own way, reinforce economic reforms. An example that springs to the mind immediately is the reservation for Other Backward Classes (OBC) in central universities and educational institutions that substantially increased the opportunities of higher education for 52 per cent of the population. That was a major reform of the UPA in 2006.

In an essay that I wrote on 29 November 2015, I had listed what I considered 'true reforms' in the modern era that began in 1991. I made a list of 11 reforms that included the Public Private Partnership (PPP) model to garner private resources for public projects and the Aadhaar-enabled DBT. Both ideas were contributed by the UPA governments.

Under 'true reforms' would fall the Fiscal Responsibility and Budget Management Act, passed by Parliament when the NDA-1 was in office but notified by the UPA-1 government. Likewise, the Value Added Tax (VAT) was implemented under UPA-1. Special Economic Zones (SEZs) were established following the passage of the SEZs Act in 2005. At end-2017, there were 222 SEZs and they gave a big push to merchandise exports that grew four-fold in 10 years. PPPs were instrumental in the aggressive expansion of capacity in airports, ports and power. The Mahatma Gandhi National Rural Employment Guarantee programme (and the Act that followed) supplemented rural-agricultural incomes, staved off hunger, and created demand in rural India. The universalisation of the Mid-day Meal Scheme had huge externalities.

Other Major Interventions

Right to Information, Right to Education and Right to Food were statutorily protected by laws made by Parliament. The National Horticulture Mission (NHM) and the Rashtriya Krishi Vikas Yojana (RKVY) boosted agricultural growth to an average of 3.7 per cent under the UPA. The National Rural Health Mission (NRHM) and the Rashtriya Swasthya Bima Yojana (RSBY) were major interventions in healthcare. The Right to Fair Compensation Act brought equity and transparency to land acquisition.

The National Disaster Management Authority Act, the Companies Act and the Lokpal and Lokayuktas Act were seminal legislation. The Women's Reservation Bill, 2008, would have dramatically transformed the polity, but it is languishing in Parliament because the UPA lacked numbers and the NDA lacks will.

The Civil Nuclear Agreement in 2008 will remain a milestone in history.

Each one of the above was a major and path-breaking reform. It is unfortunate that none of them was acknowledged by the finance minister even as he failed to acknowledge that it was the UPA that delivered the highest decadal growth since Independence. The UPA-1's record is beyond his reach in the remaining seven months, but he can try to catch up with the UPA-2's.

SHE WANTED REASONS, HERE ARE TEN

7 October 2018

The Defence Minister is an innocent person. She does not know many things that happened concerning the Rafale deal before she took over on 3 September 2017. She appears to have even overlooked her own schedule of daily engagements.

The Rafale aircraft deal between the governments of India and France was announced by the prime minister in Paris on 10 April 2015, and an agreement was signed on 23 September 2016. It has kicked up a controversy and a demand for an enquiry. Recently, the defence minister asked, 'Why should I order an enquiry?' Giving her the benefit of doubt that we always extend to innocent persons, I think it is only fair to supply the reasons. Here are 10 reasons:

1. The governments of India and France had entered into an Memorandum of Understanding (MoU) under which India would buy 126 Rafale twin-engine multi-role fighter aircraft. The price per aircraft discovered through an international bid opened on 12 December 2012, was ₹526.10 crore. Dassault, the manufacturer, would supply 18 aircraft in 'fly away' condition. The remaining 108 aircraft would be manufactured in India at the Hindustan Aeronautics Ltd's (HAL) facilities in Bengaluru using Dassault technology that would be available to HAL under a Transfer of Technology agreement. That MoU was cancelled and the prime minister announced the new 'deal' on 10 April 2015. Will the defence minister please tell us why was the decision taken to cancel the earlier MoU and enter into a new agreement?

2. Under the new agreement, India will buy 36 aircraft at an undisclosed price. The Indian Air Force has said it needed 42 squadrons of fighter jets; it has now 31 squadrons. Why did the government decide to buy only 36 aircraft (2 squadrons) when the need was for 126 aircraft (7 squadrons) and perhaps more?
3. By all accounts, the government is purchasing the same aircraft from the same manufacturer under 'the same configuration'. The last phrase is found in the joint statement dated 10 April 2015. Is it true that the price per aircraft under the new agreement is ₹1,670 crore (as disclosed by Dassault) and, if true, what is the justification for the three-fold price increase?
4. If the price of the aircraft under the new agreement is indeed 'cheaper' by 9 per cent, as claimed by the government, why is the government buying only 36 aircraft and not all the 126 aircraft offered by Dassault?
5. The new agreement was presented as an 'emergency purchase'. If the first aircraft will be delivered only in September 2019 (four years after the agreement) and the last only in 2022, how does it qualify as an emergency purchase?
6. HAL has experience of 77 years and has manufactured a variety of aircraft under licence from the respective manufacturer. When entering into the new agreement, there was no mention of Transfer of Technology from Dassault to HAL. Why was the agreement to transfer technology to HAL scrapped?
7. Every defence purchase by India imposes an 'offset' obligation upon the vendor. Dassault has admitted that it would have an offset obligation to the tune of ₹30,000 crore against the sale of 36 aircraft. HAL is a public sector undertaking. It had entered into a 'work share' agreement with Dassault on 3 March 2014, and was qualified to be the offset partner. Former President of France, Mr François Hollande, has disclosed that the Government of India had suggested the name of a private sector company as the offset partner and France and Dassault had 'no choice' in the matter. The Government of India has denied that it had suggested the name. Did the government suggest any name at

all and, if not, why did it not suggest the name of HAL?
8. The defence minister of France, Ms Florence Parly, called on the defence minister of India on 27 October 2017, in New Delhi. The same day, Ms Parly flew to Nagpur. At a function attended by Mr Nitin Gadkari, Union Minister, Mr Devendra Fadnavis, Chief Minister of Maharashtra, and the Ambassador of France to India, Ms Parly laid the foundation stone for the factory of the private sector company at Mihan, near Nagpur, where the offset supplies would be manufactured. Did the defence minister not know about this engagement of Ms Parly when the two met and, if not, did she not read about it in the newspapers the next day?
9. Dassault and the private sector offset partner had disclosed in an October 2016 press release that their joint venture 'will be a key player in the execution of offset obligations'. Was the defence minister telling the truth when she said that she was not aware if Dassault had chosen a private sector company as the offset partner?
10. HAL has a record of manufacturing MIG, Mirage and Sukhoi under licence and its own Tejas aircraft. It has assets of ₹64,000 crore. In 2017–18, its turnover was ₹18,283 crore and its profit ₹3,322 crore. In a recent statement, the defence minister has contradicted the statement of Mr T.S. Raju, former CMD of HAL, and made disparaging remarks against HAL. Is it the intention of the government to privatise HAL or close down HAL?

I have given 10 reasons (there are more) why the government should order an enquiry into the matter. Over to the innocent defence minister.

POWER LIES IN NON-USE

4 November 2018

Section 7 of the Reserve Bank of India Act, 1934 reads:

'The Central Government may from time to time give such directions to the Bank as it may, after consultation with the governor of the Bank, consider necessary in the public interest.'

The section is in the law, but the section has never been invoked. The power of the section lies in its non-use. What Parliament has told the government can be imagined as follows:

Scope of Section 7

- You are the government, but remember there is also the RBI.
- We will give you the power to issue directions but…you are obliged to consult the governor. Note, you must consult the governor, not the Bank or the Board of Directors of the Bank.
- We presume that you and the governor consult each other regularly, but remember this is a statutory consultation after your normal consultations did not result in an agreement. And when you hold the statutory consultation, please bear in mind that, under the RBI Act, it is the duty of the RBI to 'regulate the issue of bank notes and the keeping of reserves with a view to securing monetary stability'.
- At the end of the statutory consultation, you and the governor may not agree. What will you then do? Having made your point, will you leave it there and hope that, as events unfold,

the governor will change his mind? Or will you press the nuclear button and brace yourself for the inevitable fallout—the resignation of the governor?

Hostile to RBI

The above is, of course, an imaginary conversation, but that is the spirit of the law. Recent events have made it obvious that the government did not re-play the imaginary conversation in its mind when it sat down to hold regular consultations with the governor. The result is the unprecedented stand-off between the government and the RBI.

Let's recall the sequence of events.

Dr Raghuram Rajan was slighted, yet he was willing to continue beyond his initial term that ended in September 2016. He was accused of not being 'Indian enough' and virtually forced to go. Dr Urjit Patel was brought in but, within weeks, his authority was diminished by the monumental blunder called demonetisation. In global central bank circles, Dr Patel's reputation was damaged. Dr Patel tried to repair the damage by asserting his independence and authority. The government's initial concern was only about interest rates but, on that issue, Dr Patel was on a strong wicket—he had the support of the Monetary Policy Committee. Soon, the government realised that interest rate was not the only 'hurdle to growth'; other fault lines had emerged.

Take the case of the construction sector. Demonetisation had dealt a severe blow to the construction sector. Yet stock prices of real estate firms more than doubled! Since January 2018, however, stock prices of those firms have declined by 40 per cent (and by 21 per cent in the last six weeks). This is not surprising, if you consider that real estate firms turned to Non-banking Financial Companies (NBFCs) to repay their bank loans, NBFCs raised money by issuing commercial paper, and the paper was bought mainly by mutual funds and other fund-based investors. This circuit was hit by the collapse of IL&FS. Today, NBFCs are unable to raise fresh funds, sectors that depended on NBFCs for funds are squeezed, and small and medium firms that traditionally got credit from NBFCs are left in the lurch. There is fear and anger in the market.

The Fault Lines

The government is desperate to tackle three fault lines. The first is liquidity, especially the liquidity situation of NBFCs and their imminent redemption obligations. The second is the erosion of capital of public sector banks (PSBs), insufficient capital and inability to lend that has put many of them under the RBI's Prompt Corrective Action (PCA). The third is the opening of a 'special window' to provide credit to small and medium industries which were devastated by demonetisation and a flawed GST, and now hit by the NBFC crisis. It appears that the government has failed to persuade the RBI to heed its wishes.

Attempts to pressure the governor through the government's new nominees on the RBI Board also seem to have failed.

Compounding the government's misery is the growing gap between budgeted revenues and actual receipts. Having failed to 'gain' even a rupee out of demonetisation (the boast was ₹40,0,000 crore), the government has cast its eye on the reserves of the RBI. It is believed that the government asked the governor to transfer ₹100,000 crore in order to finance the budgeted expenditure and to meet the targeted fiscal deficit (FD). It is believed that the governor flatly refused. This is the spark that is about to light the powder keg.

On Wednesday, 31 October, the talk of the town in both Delhi and Mumbai was that the government will issue a directive under Section 7 on one or more issues and the governor will immediately resign in protest. Unsolicited, the government issued a statement on Wednesday that it respected the autonomy of the RBI and was holding normal consultations. If things were normal, the statement was unnecessary; if things were not normal, the statement was disingenuous!

As I conclude this essay on Friday, there is a spark and there is a powder keg. Will one be moved towards the other?

THE DAY OF RECKONING

18 November 2018

A perceptive writer has pointed out that the government and the central bank are a team in a three-legged race; they either run together or fall down.

Growth and price stability—two unexceptionable objectives of an economy—may sometimes come into conflict: when inflation is high or rising *and* the growth rate is low or sliding; or when the growth rate is too robust and threatens to push up inflation. The finance minister (government) and the governor (central bank) will take their respective positions; they will meet; each will convey his/her concerns to the other; and things will be smoothened. There is too much at stake in the governance of the country for the government and the central bank to have their daggers perpetually drawn.

Nothing like what we see today, however, has happened before. Never before has a deputy governor, encouraged by the governor to 'explore' the idea of central bank independence, delivered a public lecture to warn the government that it will incur the wrath of the markets. Never before has a finance minister retorted through another public lecture that the RBI was looking away when banks indulged in indiscriminate lending. Never before has a secretary, Economic Affairs, gloated over a temporary bump in the market and mocked the deputy governor for his dire warning.

Eyeing the Reserves

The trigger was the unprecedented invocation of Section 7 of the RBI Act, virtually commanding the governor to 'consult' with the government on certain issues of 'public interest'. The issues listed by the government were a smokescreen. Providing greater liquidity to stressed NBFCs, relaxing the rigour of PCA with respect to 11 PSBs, and a special window for providing credit to Micro, Small & Medium Enterprises (MSMEs) were not such intractable matters that the finance minister and the governor could not sit across the table and resolve them. The real issue lay behind the smokescreen—the reserves of the RBI.

The RBI's reserves as on 31 March 2018 were:

1. Currency & Gold Revaluation Reserve	₹6,91,641 crore
2. Contingency Fund	₹2,31,211 crore
3. Asset Development Fund	₹22,811 crore
4. Investment Revaluation Account	₹13,285 crore
5. Foreign Exchange Forward Contracts Valuation Account	₹3,262 crore
6. Capital Reserve	₹6,500 crore
	Total: ₹9,68,710 crore

Serial numbers 1, 4 and 5 will fluctuate depending upon the exchange rate and the interest rate. The other three are reserves built up over the years by putting away a large part of the annual surplus of the RBI. The annual surplus of the RBI has been a bone of contention between the government and the RBI. Dr Y.V. Reddy was loath to transfer the entire annual surplus to the government. Dr Raghuram Rajan resolved the issue and, beginning 2013–14, the entire annual surplus has been transferred to the government. Hence, nothing will be added to the reserves in the future from the annual surplus (although how the annual surplus is calculated could be a contested issue).

Questions, No Answers

The government seems to think that the accumulated reserves are too high. In proportion to the total assets of the RBI it is 26.8 per cent as against an average of 14 per cent for the central banks that were studied. The government is eyeing at least one-third of the reserves—approximately ₹3,20,000 crore. That sum, incidentally, resembles the sum that the government hoped to realise as a windfall out of demonetisation!

The government has a weak case and is unwilling to answer the following questions:

1. Since 2013–14, the entire annual surplus has been transferred to the government. Why is the government re-opening an issue that has been settled?
2. There is no accepted international norm regarding the optimal size of the reserves (in proportion to assets). Why does the government think that 26 per cent is too high?
3. Further, is the situation in India (exchange rate volatility, inflation, capital flows) comparable to the situation in the countries that were studied?
4. Has the government examined Section 47 of the RBI Act that reads 'the balance of the profits shall be paid to the Central Government'?
5. Since the government has claimed that its fiscal math for 2018–19 is correct and it is on course to achieve the FD target, why does the government need the money this year?
6. What was the government doing in the last four years and six months and what is the tearing hurry to 'fix the economic capital framework of the RBI' towards the end of its term? Should not the issue be left to the next government?

Fixing What's Not Broke

The sensible course for the government and the RBI is to put aside the issue of reserves and focus on the immediate concerns. It is not difficult for both to agree on a course of action concerning liquidity for NBFCs, revision of PCA norms, forbearance in the case of selected sectors (like power) burdened by NPAs, generous credit to MSMEs, etc. Each one is simply a matter of numbers and finding optimal solutions.

However, if the government is intent on 'fixing' the capital framework of the RBI, then its motives are dishonest. The inescapable conclusion will be that the government's aim is to force Dr Urjit Patel to resign, appoint a pliant governor, and convert the RBI into a conventional Board-managed company. That is why I had said that 19 November 2018 will be a day of reckoning for central bank independence and the Indian economy.

ANOTHER INSTITUTION IS FALLING

25 November 2018

The readers/viewers are spoilt for choice. There is the pre-scheduled India vs Australia series of cricket matches. There is Central Bureau of Investigation (CBI) vs CBI. And the latest blockbuster is Government vs RBI.

Every cricket player has his share of bruises, the CBI is broken and, in the case of the RBI, it has been severely bent.

The RBI is the central bank for India. Most people do not know or understand the critical role played by the central bank in the governance of a country. The main objective of a central bank is to secure monetary stability. The objectives of the RBI Act, 1934, are 'to regulate the issue of bank notes and the keeping of reserves with a view to securing monetary stability'.

RBI Has Many Roles

The RBI has several functions. It creates money. It issues currency notes. It sets the interest rates. It exchanges currency. It regulates transactions involving foreign exchange. It keeps the reserves. It manages the debt of the government. It licences and regulates commercial banks and non-banking finance companies. Many of its responsibilities are directly connected to the paramount objective of 'securing monetary stability'.

The RBI's core responsibilities are not different from the responsibilities of central banks of other countries that have an open economy. The premise on which a central bank stands ready and able to discharge its responsibilities is 'central bank independence'. The Charter of the European Central Bank (ECB) states, *inter alia*, 'neither the ECB, nor a national central bank, nor any member of their decision-making bodies shall seek or take instructions from Union institutions, bodies, offices or agencies, from any government of a Member State or from any other body'.

The principle of central bank independence is now virtually an immutable law. Therefore, although the RBI was constituted under an Act of Parliament, the RBI is not—and cannot be treated like—a board-managed company. Everywhere in the world, central bank = governor (or chairman). Everything that is done under the Act, therefore, has to be consistent with the underlying premise of the Act; otherwise it would be *ultra vires*. It is this principle of central bank independence that has been challenged by the NDA government.

Independence Challenged

On 19 November 2018, the principle was severely tested—and breached. At a meeting of the Board of Directors of the RBI, four decisions were taken:

- The Board *decided* to constitute an expert committee to examine the Economic Capital Framework (ECF), the membership and ToR of which will be jointly *determined* by the government and the RBI;
- The Board *advised* that the RBI should consider a scheme of restructuring of stressed standard assets of MSME borrowers with exposure up to ₹25 crore;
- The Board *decided* to retain capital adequacy ratio (CAR) at 9 per cent and agreed to extend the transition period by one year; and
- The Board *decided* that the issue regarding banks under the PCA Framework will be examined by the Board of Financial Supervision of the RBI.

In my view, it was a disastrous meeting that cut a dangerous new path. On three of four matters, the Board took *decisions*. Once the government had drawn blood, it stepped back from actually invoking Section 7 (to issue Directions) or Section 58 (to make Regulations). Nevertheless, it is clear that the camel has its nose in the tent; it is only a matter of time before it has its trunk and feet inside.

I have no reservation in believing that most of the independent directors on the Board are distinguished professionals or successful businesspersons in their respective field or fields. However, none of them was, or is, a central banker and none of them has domain knowledge of central bank functions. Besides, from many accounts of the meeting, it can be inferred that the independent directors were not independent of the government that appointed them; they seem to have enthusiastically supported the government's position. The same Board had failed the country when it meekly endorsed demonetisation on 8 November 2016. Now, after two years and ten days, the Board has once again failed the country by breaching central bank independence.

Accountable, Not Subordinate

It is par for the course for the finance minister and the governor to agree (more often) or disagree (occasionally) on the repo rate or Cash Reserve Ratio (CRR). I am in favour of some tension between the government and the governor and occasionally in favour of the government expressing its disappointment occasionally. I am in favour of Parliament calling the governor more frequently to explain his actions before a committee. I am in favour of academics and the media fearlessly criticising the governor's decisions. However, I strongly disapprove of government-appointed directors deciding issues that fall within the jurisdiction of the central bank/governor. Whether they do so 'independently' or on the 'instructions' of the government is immaterial; in either case it is an encroachment and will destroy the fundamental principle of central bank independence.

At the next meeting of the Board on 14 December 2018, there

will certainly be a determined push by the government to make the Board decide on more issues. If Dr Urjit Patel does not stand his ground, and yields more space, another institution—a venerable one—would have fallen. For the present, I shall utter a prayer and keep my fingers crossed.

THE FAMILIAR SOUND OF THE DRUMS

2 December 2018

Mr Narendra Modi has come a long way since 2013–14. Candidate Modi was all about *vikas* (development). The bulk of the 31 per cent of the electorate that voted for the BJP in May 2014 was swayed by the slogan *Sabka Saath, Sabka Vikas* (Together with All, Development for All). There was another catchy slogan: *Achhe Din Aane Wale Hain* (Good Days Are Coming). Then there were the promises: ₹15 lakh in the bank account of every citizen; 2 crore jobs a year; doubling the income of the farmer; minimum government, maximum governance; the rupee trading at ₹40 to a dollar; a fitting (and final) reply to Pakistan; and many others.

Prime Minister Modi kept up the rhetoric. In his first Independence Day address on 15 August 2014, he proposed a moratorium of 10 years on all divisive issues. His exact words were:

'We have had enough of fights, many have been killed. Friends, look behind and you will find that nobody has benefited from it. Except casting a slur on Mother India, we have done nothing. Therefore, I appeal to all those people that whether it is the poison of casteism, communalism, regionalism, discrimination on social and economic basis, all these are obstacles in our way forward. Let's resolve for once in our hearts, let's put a moratorium on all such activities for 10 years, we shall march ahead to a society which will be free from all such tensions.'

Great Start, Sharp Slide

That was a great start. Many thought Mr Modi would be Prime Minister of Everybody. Alas, he did not remain true to his word. He did not put down with an iron hand the depredations of *gau rakshak* vigilantes. He did not stop the activities of anti-Romeo squads, *ghar wapsi* groups or *khap* panchayats. The prime minister did not go on air and publicly condemn such impunity. The result was growing mob violence, lynchings and so-called honour killings. Average, decent people began to lose faith in him.

Although the prime minister refused to hold press conferences, and the BJP had successfully tamed vast sections of the media, got editors and anchors sacked and ushered in the era of 'handout journalism', questions were raised in the media and critical editorials and op-eds continued to appear. Moreover, nothing could stop the intrepid social media from holding a mirror to the BJP-led government.

Markets Are Merciless

The prime minister also greatly underestimated the power of the market. It is the market that first called out the prime minister and his government. Markets do not like crude disruptions such as demonetisation. Apart from the enormous pain and suffering that it imposed on millions of people and businesses, demonetisation caused grave uncertainty, and markets dislike uncertainty and unpredictability in government's policy actions. When demonetisation was followed by a poorly designed and inefficiently implemented GST, the markets punished the policymakers for their incompetence.

What followed was inevitable: flight of capital, slowdown in investment, rise of Non-performing Assets (NPAs), deceleration in credit growth, stagnation of exports, farm sector distress, and exploding unemployment.

During this period, the BJP suffered a severe setback in Bihar. Although it scored a thumping victory in Uttar Pradesh and

Uttarakhand, it lost in Punjab, Goa and Manipur. The BJP got its worst drubbing in a string of by-elections, including in states where it was the ruling party.

In my view, after being check-mated in Karnataka, Mr Modi decided to shed the garb of Prime Minister of Everybody. He did not even become, once again, Candidate Modi, because the promises made by the BJP had become objects of ridicule and that option was ruled out. Mr Modi seems to have decided to go back further in time and don the mantle of Hindu *Hriday Samrat* (Emperor of Hindu Hearts), which was his USP in Gujarat.

Law for Temple Chorus

The *sarsanghchalak* (chief) of the RSS, Mr Mohan Bhagwat, blew the bugle when he called for a law to build a Ram temple on the disputed site at Ayodhya, notwithstanding the case pending in the Supreme Court. Taking the cue, every Hindutva organisation has demanded a law. Some have demanded an ordinance. A BJP MP has promised to move a private member's Bill. The Shiv Sena has dared the government to bring an ordinance. A Dharma Sabha was convened on 25 November to demand a law. It was announced that the date for commencement of construction of the temple would be announced at the *Kumbh Mela* on 1 February 2019.

The president of the BJP has thrown helpful hints. Mr Narendra Modi has maintained a deafening silence. There is a pattern to these actions. Everyone knows that nothing stirs in the BJP without the direction of Mr Modi, no Hindutva organization moves without the nod of the RSS, and no major decision is taken by the RSS and BJP without an agreement between Mr Bhagwat and Mr Modi.

One can pray to Lord Ram before an election and seek his blessing. One can pray to Lord Ram after an election and offer thanks. But when the BJP places its total faith in Lord Ram to win the election, it is a confession that the people have lost faith in the BJP.

RAFALE JUDGMENT AND THE UNAVOIDABLE OPTION

23 December 2018

A judgment is an authority for what it decides—the ratio—and not for what may logically follow from the decision. That's a settled principle of law.

In the case of Manohar Lal Sharma vs Narendra Damodardas Modi and other cases (*the Rafale Deal cases*) the judgment of the Supreme Court pronounced on 14 December 2018, will be remembered more for the questions that the Court did not decide than for the questions that were decided.

The Court's approach was pretty simple and straightforward: there are severe limits to the Court's jurisdiction while examining a case of defence procurement. Lest the point was lost on the average reader, the Court concluded the judgment with the following words: 'We however make it clear that our views as above are primarily from the standpoint of the exercise of jurisdiction under Article 32 of the Constitution of India which has been invoked in the present group of cases.'

Limits of Jurisdiction

The lesson is clear: the petitioners erred in invoking the jurisdiction of the Supreme Court under Article 32 of the Constitution. Practically every conclusion declining to examine or decide the key issues in dispute followed from the conclusion regarding the jurisdictional limits of the Court.

'It was also made clear that the issue of pricing or matters relating to technical suitability of the equipment would not be gone into by the Court.' (Para 12)

'We are satisfied that there is no occasion to really doubt the process, and even if minor deviations have occurred, that would not result in either setting aside the contract or requiring a detailed scrutiny by the Court.' (Para 22)

'We cannot sit in judgement over the wisdom of deciding to go in for purchase of 36 aircraft in place of 126.' (Para 22)

'It is certainly not the job of this Court to carry out a comparison of the pricing details in matters like the present.' (Para 26)

'...it is neither appropriate nor within the experience of this Court to step into this arena of what is technically feasible or not.' (Para 33)

Precisely for the reasons given by the Supreme Court, the Court ought to have, at the threshold, declined to entertain the petitions.

Dubious Claims/Statements

There is another aspect of the judgment that is unusual. The Court seems to have 'accepted' whatever the government had stated either in the note in the sealed cover or in the oral arguments. Sample the following: that withdrawal of the original Request for Proposal (RFP) was initiated in March 2015; that the contract negotiations between Dassault and HAL could not be concluded on account of unresolved issues; that the Indian Negotiating Team had arrived at better terms relating to price, delivery and maintenance; the processes had been followed; a redacted version of the Comptroller and Auditor General's (CAG's) report was placed before Parliament and the report of the CAG has been examined by the PAC; the Chief of Air Staff communicated his reservation regarding the disclosure of the pricing details; the pricing details are covered by Article 10 of the Inter-Governmental Agreement(IGA) between the two governments; there is a commercial advantage in the purchase of 36 Rafale aircraft; there were certain better terms in IGA qua maintenance and weapon package; Dassault was circumspect about HAL carrying out the contractual obligations; Dassault has signed partnership agreements with several companies and is negotiating with over hundred; there was possibly an agreement between the parent Reliance company and Dassault starting from the year 2012; and there has been a categorical denial from every side of the interview given by the former president of France, Mr Francois Hollande. None of these statements/claims is entirely true and the Court, owing to its limited jurisdiction, did not examine their veracity. So, who can? The obvious answer is that only a parliamentary inquiry will expose the falsity of the statements/claims and bring out the truth.

The forbearance shown by the Court has led the Court to commit an egregious error. There is no report of the CAG yet; no version of the report, redacted or otherwise, has been placed before Parliament; and the report has not been shared with or examined by the PAC. After misleading the Court, the government has conveniently blamed the Court for 'misinterpreting' its note! The government has also given lessons in English grammar to the Court! Those are the perils of adopting the 'sealed cover' approach.

Unanswered Questions

There are at least three big questions that can be answered only by a parliamentary inquiry.

- Why did the government scrap the transfer of technology agreement and work share agreement (13 March 2014) between Dassault and HAL when 95 per cent of the negotiations had been completed between the two (Dassault CEO, 28 March 2015 and foreign secretary, 8 April 2015)?
- If the new price is cheaper by 9 to 20 per cent, why did the government not buy the 126 aircraft offered by Dassault, since the Air Force desperately needs to augment its fleet of fighter aircraft?
- Why did the government not push the case of HAL, the only

company that has manufactured aircraft in India, for the whole or part of the Offset contracts?

Notwithstanding the judgment of the Supreme Court, there are unverified claims and unanswered questions. The judgment has, by default, made a parliamentary inquiry unavoidable. Over to the people's court.

THE YEAR ENDS ON A SOMBRE NOTE

30 December 2018

Democracy is all about balance. When the balance is threatened or affected, the survival of democracy is put into question. India finds itself at a stage where the question—Will democracy survive in India?—looms large.

Each one of the issues that I shall examine in this essay may, by itself, not appear to be a threat to democracy and may appear remediable. However, if a remedy is not found, even one issue can derail democracy. If many of the issues remain unresolved, I am certain that democracy—as it is understood in free, liberal and mature nations—will perish.

Elections

On the day after the results of the elections were announced in Telangana, the Chief Electoral Officer of the state (a nominee of the Central Election Commission [CEC]) 'apologized' for the deletion of 22 lakh voters from the electoral rolls (amounting to 8 per cent of the official number of electors of 283 lakh). A cool apology and end of story. In a vigilant democracy, all political parties would have come together and brought millions of people on the streets to protest the scandal. The CEO would have resigned or been sacked. The officials of the CEC who supervised the revision of the electoral rolls in Telangana would have been suspended. None of that happened, and nobody is outraged. Life goes on in Telangana under a democratically elected chief minister.

Legislatures

Take a look at the table, the gender imbalance is pronounced, and it seems nobody is serious about creating a gender-equal society.

State	Elected MLAs	Women MLAs
Chhattisgarh	90	13
Rajasthan	199	23
Madhya Pradesh	230	22
Telangana	119	6
Mizoram	40	0

Every party must share the blame. They field few women candidates, preferring men on the ground of 'winnability', or nominate women as candidates in constituencies where the party has little chance of winning. Few women MLAs means few women ministers; there is none in Mizoram because the winner, the Mizo National Front (MNF), fielded no woman candidate! The solution is simple: reserve at least 33 per cent of the seats in legislatures for women. It is not a revolutionary idea because such reservation is already the law in elections to municipalities and panchayats.

Courts

The court system has broken down, and it is doubtful if it can be put together as a whole within a reasonable time. The problem is not confined to vacancies, it is much larger. The other aspects of the broken system are the outdated and dysfunctional procedures, lack of infrastructure, non-use of modern technology, unqualified men and women impersonating lawyers, the unwillingness or inability of Bar Councils to throw the imposters out, and widely prevalent corruption at all levels. If justice is still rendered in many cases, that is despite the system and thanks to good, conscientious judges. The alarming fact is, that tribe is not increasing.

Public Interest Litigation (PIL)

What was encouraged as a tool to bring justice to the 'poor and oppressed who have no access to the courts' has turned into a malevolent instrument to 'fix' outcomes and short-circuit the normal legal processes. The motives of some PIL petitioners are suspect. Novel procedures of questionable validity have been adopted by courts while adjudicating PILs. In the process, the higher courts have clutched at jurisdiction, usurped the powers of the Executive government and even encroached upon the territory of the legislatures/Parliament. It may seem that 'justice has been done' in the case at hand, but actually grave damage is done to the procedure established by law as well as to the settled principles of law. In some cases, the judgments are manifestly wrong.

Bureaucracy

The greatest failure of our administrations has been the inability to execute projects and programmes and deliver the promised outcomes/benefits. On rare occasions, the administration has risen to the challenge (such as relief in the case of a disaster), but, more often, the people are thoroughly dissatisfied. While elected politicians are constructively responsible, the direct responsibility is with the bureaucracy. Civil servants design the projects and programmes, they make cost and time estimates, and they are directly responsible for implementation; yet, many programmes have failed completely and many others have yielded unsatisfactory results. There is abundant talent in the country, but such talent is serving the private sector or in foreign countries. We have found no answer to the problem, which is only getting worse as the years pass by.

Institutions, Organizations

Never before have so many bodies been so badly damaged in so short a time as in the last four years. The CEC, Central Information

Commission (CIC) and RBI have been undermined or compromised. The CBI has imploded; a change of government will cause more investigating agencies to implode.

Taxation

In normal times, tax rates must be moderate and tax administration a service. Those rules have been turned upside down. Now, tax rates are extortionate and discriminatory (e.g. GST) and tax administration is tax terrorism.

Prime Minister

The current prime minister is not the head of the government, he *is* the government. Without a Constitutional amendment, a parliamentary democracy has been converted into an almost-presidential government. All checks and balances have been eliminated.

A dysfunctional democracy will perish. Democracy will survive in India only if we restore the balance. Let me end the year on an optimistic note: 'If winter comes, can spring be far behind?'

ECONOMY

The economy continued to cause concern. The BJP did not seem to have learned any lessons from the disaster of demonetization and the flawed implementation of the GST. In fact, the government seemed willing to reverse the process of liberalization. Distinguished economists left the government in disgust or despair. Most analysts and observers were left with the impression that the management of the economy was in the hands of not very competent persons. It was no surprise that all the economic indicators were unsatisfactory and the growth rate—despite being boosted by the new methodology—remained modest.

TRUTH, POST-TRUTH AND AGAIN THE TRUTH

14 January 2018

As Parliament's delayed Winter Session was nearing an end, the finance minister found himself in an awkward situation. On 4 January 2018, the Rajya Sabha had listed a short duration discussion on the state of the economy and he was required to reply. Twenty-seven days before the Budget, it was an awkward time to speak extensively on the state of the economy or to give any assurances. The truth about the economy is known to everyone. Mr Jaitley's reply was the post-truth. I think it is necessary to state the truth once again.

Growth Rate, Fiscal Deficit

1. FM: 'Over the last three-and-a-half to four years, the government has taken several steps to ensure that the decision-making process with regard to economy is in the interest of both public and economy and remains reliable.'

The decision-making process of the NDA government was either opaque (demonetisation) or erratic (GST). Given the many instances of reneging on promises, certainly, there was no reliability. The result is the slowdown, now admitted, reluctantly, by the government. In the seven quarters beginning January 2016, the quarterly growth rate of Gross Value Added (GVA) was 8.7, 7.6, 6.8, 6.7, 5.6, 5.6 and 6.1 per cent. In the same period, the growth of GDP had declined from 9.1 to 6.3 per cent and IIP remained almost stationary between 121.4 and 120.9.

2. FM: 'You have expressed concern whether fiscal deficit can have slippage. Today, we get the concern about marginal slippage… Your fiscal deficit was nearing 6 per cent.'

After the international financial crisis of 2008, the UPA government increased public expenditure and allowed the FD to rise to 5.9 per cent in 2011–12. In the next two years it was brought down to 4.9 and 4.5 per cent (as on 31 March 2014). The NDA will bring it down to 3.2 per cent as on 31 March 2018. Both are commendable reductions—1.4 per cent by the UPA in two years and 1.3 per cent by the NDA in four years. When the finance minister achieves his FD target at the end of 2017–18, I shall compliment him.

Doing Business, Exports

3. FM: 'You had left the country at 142nd rank in "Ease of Doing Business" in a total of 168 countries. If we come to 100th place from 142, you think the other way, you know its impact.'

India's rank was 134/183 in 2011 (UPA) and 142/189 in 2015 (NDA). In 2017 it rose to 130/189. That is good news, although it is based on surveys in only two cities and attributable to improvements in two parameters. However, the 'impact' is doubtful. Look at two metrics:

	2016–17 (NDA)	2013–14 (UPA)
Investment proposals (CMIE), in ₹crore:	7,90,000	16,20,000
Stalled projects (number):	926 (Sep 2017)	766

4. FM: 'It is natural that when economy of the world would be weak, there would be less purchasing by buyers, exports would be slow. But this year data of export is getting changed.'

Here are the figures. There is no direct correlation between world growth rate and value of merchandise exports. Even when world growth rate improved, India's merchandise exports remained below USD 300 billion. There is no explanation.

Year	World Growth, Calendar Year (as per IMF, in %)	India's Merchandise Exports (in USD billion)
UPA		
2010–11	5.4	250
2011–12	4.3	306
2012–13	3.5	300
2013–14	3.5	314
NDA		
2014–15	3.6	310
2015–16	3.4	262
2016–17	3.2	274
2017–18	3.6	170 (Apr–Oct)

Investments, NPAs

5. FM: 'Capital formation, on the basis of which you said public investment was challenging, was pertaining to the data of the last quarter… It has started nearing 4.7 per cent, in the positive territory again, and similarly the data pertaining to non-food credit is between 10 and 11 per cent.'

GFCF has steadily declined since Q1 of 2014–15 (32.2 per cent). It touched a low of 28.9 per cent in Q2 of 2017–18. Credit growth has been sluggish since Q1 of 2014–15 (12.9 per cent). It touched a low of 5.4 per cent in Q4 of 2016–17 and recovered to 6.5 per cent in Q2 of 2017–18. Do the Q2 numbers point to a recovery? Obviously, it is too early to reach a conclusion. One swallow does not make a summer.

6. FM: 'That is why a huge recapitalization plan has been made and therefore we have enhanced the ability of these banks.'

The NPA data is self-explanatory. NPAs have jumped from ₹2,63,372 crore in 2013–14 to ₹7,76,087 crore by 30 September 2017. After 43 months in office, no issue can be termed as a legacy issue. There has been no explanation so far why loans that were performing as on 31 March 2014 became non-performing in the last four years.

The Truth

The truth is that the economy is poorly managed, not able to attract investments and not able to create jobs. The post-truth is that the economy is the fastest or second fastest growing economy in the world and therefore 'we are the best'. The truth, again, is that 2017–18 will end with 6.5 per cent growth, maybe even lower; and 2018–19 will be a challenging year for prices, investments and jobs, leaving the people to ask, 'What did we get in the last five years?'

THE 70 LAKH BOAST

28 January 2018

Prof. Pulak Ghosh and Dr Soumya Kanti Ghosh are respected academics. They created a minor storm recently when they claimed that 70 lakh new 'payroll' jobs will be created in India in the organized sector in 2017–18.

The authors explained that 'payroll' job is a job where the employee has enrolled under the Employees' Provident Fund Organisation (EPFO) or Employees' State Insurance Corporation (ESIC) or National Pension Scheme (NPS) or Government Provident Fund (GPF). Enrolment under one of the four schemes is certainly evidence that the employee is on the payroll of an employer—private sector or public sector or government or parastatal body.

Seventy lakh new jobs is a claim that will take one's breath away. In the same article, the authors reported that the total 'payroll' stock as on 31 March 2017, was 919 lakh. So, it has taken the country 70 years to create a 'payroll' stock of 919 lakh jobs but, miraculously, in just 12 months, the country will generate 70 lakh new 'payroll' jobs—that is nearly 7.5 per cent of the current stock!

The EPFO Surprise

The largest subset of the stock of 'payroll' jobs is EPFO-enrolled jobs. The authors reported that the 'EPFO manages a corpus of over ₹11 lakh crore for its estimated 550 lakh subscribers across jurisdictions in over 190 industries employing more than 20+ people'. According to the authors, 45.4 lakh new subscribers in the age band 18–25 years had enrolled under the EPFO in 2016–17 and started making their monthly contributions to the Fund. They also found that 36.8 lakh new subscribers in the same age band had enrolled between April and November 2017 and, therefore, they estimated that, for the full year 2017–18, 55.2 lakh new subscribers would be enrolled.

If **industries/businesses** in the **organized sector** that employed **20 or more persons** can generate in a year 55 lakh new jobs that **qualified for enrolment** under the EPFO alone, then we can declare that India has, truly and comprehensively, slain the demon of unemployment!

To the above jobs we must add:

- New jobs in businesses in the organized sector that employed less than 20 persons;
- New jobs in the unorganized or unregulated sector—this will include micro and small enterprises (running into millions);
- New jobs in the farm sector;
- New casual and temporary jobs such as loader, courier, messenger, etc.;
- New jobs in the illegitimate economy.

If we assume that for every 'payroll' job counted by the authors there will be another job created in the sectors that I have listed above, then the count will rise to 140 lakh in 2017–18. According to the Ghoshs' report, 150 lakh persons enter the labour force every year of which 66 lakh is skilled manpower. Soon, the problem will not be lack of jobs but lack of jobseekers! (By way of comparison, China, which has a GDP five times that of India's, adds about 150 lakh jobs a year.)

Hence, the crucial numbers that must be validated are the new EPFO-enrolled jobs—45.4 lakh in 2016–17 and 55.2 lakh in 2017–18. If these numbers are valid, the claim of 70 lakh new 'payroll' jobs in 2017–18 may be accepted.

The Dissent

Mr Jairam Ramesh and Mr Praveen Chakravarthy are also respected academics.

The two of them, in a jointly authored article, questioned the Ghoshs' report. They argued that a new registration in any year did not mean a new job was created in that year; it could mean that an informal job was formalized and a non-subscriber became a subscriber in that year. According to them, demonetisation forced formalisation of jobs post-November 2016 and the GST forced formal registration of businesses post-July 2017, and the formalisation happened in 2017–18. (While formalisation was a gain, demonetisation and the GST also caused job losses and closure of thousands of small and micro businesses.) They also pointed out that the limited data available in the public domain indicated that the number of contributing members in the EPFO grew by 7 per cent in 2014–15 and 8 per cent in 2015–16 but, according to the Ghoshs' report, the number jumped by 20 per cent in 2016–17 and by a further 23 per cent up to December 2017!

Prof Ghosh and Dr Ghosh posted a reply to the criticism. They asserted that they had counted only first-time employees and had taken care to delete a large number of EPFO account-holders who did not satisfy the strict criteria. The only concession they were willing to make was that the number of 70 lakh was a gross figure that included vacancies that were filled after the incumbent had retired.

Two Demands

The debate stands at an interesting stage. It is evident that the Ghoshs were given privileged access to data that is not in the public domain. So,

- Firstly, the government must put all the EPFO subscriber data in the public domain;
- Secondly, Prof. Ghosh and Dr Ghosh must apply the same methodology and compute the number of EPFO-enrolled new

jobs that were created in 2014–15 and 2015–16, the two NDA years before demonetisation and the GST. They should go further and compute the numbers for the UPA years (2004–2014) as well.

It is only a time series of data that will reveal the truth. Otherwise, the 70 lakh jobs claim will remain a boast and, in course of time, be regarded as a bluff.

WHAT HAPPENED TO INDRADHANUSH?

25 February 2018

Are PSBs wanted or not wanted? The answer seems to depend on the day of the week.

Since nationalization of major banks, the contributions of PSBs have been widely acknowledged.

- PSBs led the drive towards opening more bank branches, especially in rural areas. Today, there are 1,16,394 branches of all banks, of which 33,864 are in rural areas.
- PSBs expanded agricultural credit. Short term agricultural credit ('crop loans') in 2017–18 will amount to ₹6,22,685 crore.
- PSBs pioneered the concept of priority sector lending. Otherwise, many sectors would have been deprived of bank credit. Differential Rate of Interest (DRI) loans to the very poor was a plan implemented by PSBs.
- PSBs extended loans to women's self-help groups. PSBs gave education loans. Last reported outstanding amounts under the two categories were ₹61,600 crore and ₹70,400 crore respectively.
- PSBs funded rural infrastructure through the Rural Infrastructure Development Fund.
- PSBs pioneered financial inclusion. When the UPA demitted office, there were 24.3 crore 'no frills' new accounts. The NDA claims 31.11 crore Jan Dhan accounts have been opened.

Not Black and White

India's policy on the banking sector has evolved over the years. From a sole PSB (State Bank of India) to bank nationalization to competition (PSBs, private banks and foreign banks) to diluting the government's holding to not less than 55 per cent to licencing more private sector banks to privatizing a PSB (UTI Bank was converted to Axis Bank), banking policy has run a full course.

In comparison to private banks, PSBs fall short on many financial ratios, market capitalization, and management competence. Yet, there is a widely held view, especially among the middle classes and the poor—not without justification—that PSBs must be nurtured. Several straw polls have revealed that the majority opinion is against privatizing PSBs.

The scandal involving the PNB has revived the demand for privatization as part of comprehensive banking sector reforms. As a general proposition, a scam has nothing to do with ownership. Much larger bank scams have occurred in private banks in many countries. In the last ten years alone, private banks such as Lehman Brothers, Royal Bank of Scotland and Merrill Lynch have collapsed due to scandals.

Regulatory Failure

PSBs in India have multiple layers of supervision. It starts with the Board of Directors. Then there are the RBI (the regulator-cum-supervisor), the Department of Financial Services and the NDA government's creation called Bank Board Bureau. The All India Bank Officers' Association has pointed out that a PSB branch is 'subject to seven audits—internal audit, concurrent audit, snap audit, recovery audit, statutory audit, external audit and stock audit'.

Among the auditors are the firms empanelled by the CAG and the Big Four firms of chartered accountants!

It would be incorrect to say that the troubles of PSBs began with the NDA government, but it is fair to ask what the NDA government has done, since 2014, to improve governance of banks.

Soon after assuming office, the NDA government separated the offices of Chairperson and Managing Director of a PSB. It made arbitrary and whimsical transfers among the chairpersons. It changed the rules and appointed two outsiders as Managing Directors of two important PSBs. Within days, it changed the rules again, and reverted to the old rule of promoting Executive Directors as Managing Directors!

In 2015, amidst great fanfare, the government announced the Indradhanush plan to reform PSBs. In true BJP-style, the reforms were listed in a nice alphabetical order: A for Appointments; B for Bank Board Bureau and so on up to G for Governance Reforms.

Mr S.S. Mundra retired as deputy governor, RBI, in July 2017. He was in charge of the Department of Banking Supervision. The post, by convention held by a banker, remains vacant till date!

Clueless and Helpless

The government fussed over recapitalization of banks and declared that it would give funds only to those banks that undertook reforms. The PNB was given ₹4,714 crore since 2014–15 and was promised ₹5,473 crore more! No one will answer the question how it qualified for recapitalization money.

On the question what has the present government done to reform PSBs, the evidence says precious little. Here are three pieces of evidence:

- The massive fraud in PNB, and perhaps in other banks too, indicates that little has changed in the systems of PSBs.
- After Indradhanush the government got into the habit of announcing reforms that were nothing more than attractive slogans and acronyms. So, we have Enhanced Access and Service Excellence (EASE) and a 'Seven-pronged Approach'. No one knows if Indradhanush was fired at all or it misfired!
- In the light of the PNB fraud, all that the finance minister

could tell the country (after several days of silence) was that he was anguished over the 'lack of ethics' among bankers and auditors and promised to punish the perpetrators so that such 'stray cases' do not occur again. Stray cases? It is evident that the government has run out of ideas—and acronyms too.

A reform is a plan that is conceived, well-designed and implemented with a clear focus on the intended outcomes. It will take time, say five years, which is why the term of a government is five years. The last four years were wasted and the fifth too is likely to be wasted.

THE ONE-TRICK PONY IN DELHI

29 April 2018

The first Gulf War 1990 was fought on oil: which companies will control the oil fields of the Arabian region? Norway wisely built a Future Fund on oil revenues, strict control on its use and fiscal discipline. Latin American economies flourished or perished on their use of oil revenues. Venezuela is broke despite having some of the largest known oil reserves. For many years, Russia made its annual budget assuming that crude oil prices will be USD 100 or above. When oil prices collapsed, the Russian economy also collapsed.

Enjoying the Bonanza

Oil is a critical factor in any economy. India's dependence on oil imports is 80 per cent. When crude oil prices collapsed in 2014 and brought a windfall, the central budget was based on low prices. Low oil prices gave room to the BJP-NDA government and state governments to tax the consumer to the hilt and garner large resources without fuelling inflation. On the expenditure side, the allocation for subsidies on LPG, kerosene and fertilisers could be reduced. The government also saved on expenditure on Railways and in other departments. Altogether, it was a good time for the government: it reaped a windfall without sparing a thought for what it would do when oil prices rose again.

Look at the revenues collected by the central government and state governments in recent years from taxes on petrol and diesel (see Table):

Year	Central Government			State Governments		
	₹Per Litre Petrol	₹Per Litre Diesel	Total contribution (₹crores)	₹Per Litre Petrol	₹Per Litre Diesel	Total Contribution (₹crores)
2013–14	10.38	4.52	152900	11.90	6.41	152460
2014–15	18.14	10.91	172066	11.05	6.06	160554
2015–16	19.56	11.16	258443	12.14	6.79	160209
2016–17	21.99	17.83	334534	13.95	7.99	189770
2017–18 (est)	20.06	15.92	230807 (Apr–Dec'17)	14.07	8.53	150996 (Apr–Dec'17)

The flip side was increased dependence on taxes on petroleum and petroleum products. The central government's receipts from such taxes as a percentage of total revenue receipts have steadily increased from 15 per cent in 2013–14 to 24 per cent in 2016–17. On the contrary, state governments' receipts from taxes on the petroleum sector as a percentage of total revenue receipts have moderated from 10 per cent in 2013–14 to 8 per cent in 2016–17.

Tax and Spend Failed

The BJP-NDA government bought the strategy of 'tax and spend'. Government expenditure increased sharply in the years 2014–15 to 2016–17. It was believed that expenditure-led growth will crowd-in private investments. That did not happen. Despite various slogans—Make in India, Start Up India, etc—private investment is not taking place. GFCF has fallen from 31.30 per cent in 2013–14 to 28.49 per cent in 2017–18. Of this, private capital formation has fallen from 24.20 per cent to 21.38 per cent (upto 2016–17). Start Up India is a non-starter. Official data revealed that only 109 out of 6,981 recognized start-up businesses had received government support/funding.

There were alternatives. A bold move to cut taxes on petrol

and diesel would have given a big boost to private consumption. A cut in taxes would have led to cost savings and competitive pricing for exporters and would have boosted exports. Both would have resulted in benefits to industry: higher capacity utilisation, enhanced productivity and more employment.

Alternative approaches were either not explored or shunned. Why? I can only put it down to the lack of collective thinking and collective decision-making. When one person rides into town on a white horse and claims to have answers to all the problems of the country, and will not listen to advice or brook dissent, the result is what is called a 'one-trick pony'. Government expenditure-led growth was the Gujarat model. Undeniably, that model has worked in some countries when there was a recession. But, India in May 2014 did not face a recession. According to the government's own figures, the economy grew by 6.4 per cent in 2013-14. A great opportunity to boost the growth rate was lost.

No Options Left

The experience of the last four years is that the Gujarat model has not worked. At the end of the second year, the government should have shifted gears. It did not. The problem was compounded when the GST was introduced on 1 July 2017. Brushing aside advice, the government stuck to high and multiple rates of GST, pushing industry—especially MSMEs—into a struggle for survival. The double blow of demonetisation and a flawed GST knocked out the confidence of investors.

The burden of high taxes on petroleum and diesel is borne by the people. They do so silently—what choice do they have?—but not willingly. Ask owners of two-wheelers, cars, taxis, autos, tractors and commercial trucks. Every time they fill the tank, they curse the central government. When petrol and diesel prices hit an all-time high last week, the voices of protest grew louder. The demand for bringing petroleum and petroleum products under GST is gaining support.

As the government enters the last year of its term, it has few options. The fiscal space has reduced considerably. It is deeply committed to the 'tax and spend' strategy and it will be difficult to unwind that strategy in the final year. As the price of crude oil rises, the government is clueless and floundering. The prognosis, therefore, is crushing taxes, higher prices and greater burden on the average consumer. Curse and bear it.

WHO IS MINDING THE STORE?

27 May 2018

While you were absorbed in the designed-to-be-nail-biting IPL cricket matches and the game of thrones in Karnataka, something happened to the economy. It is time that we dragged the government by the collar and asked them to attend to the issues that are gravely challenging the economy.

Current Account Deficit (CAD)

The CAD was a major challenge in 2012–13. Through hard measures, it was brought down to 1.74 per cent in 2013–14. A dramatic collapse in oil prices helped the NDA government to boast that they had wrought a miracle in the first three years. Now, when the tide has turned, government has no answers.

The CAD in 2017–18 was 1.9 per cent (likely) and for 2018–19 the estimate is 2.5 per cent.

Depreciating Rupee

A famous election promise was that the rupee-dollar rate (then ₹59) will be brought down to ₹40! Between January and May 2018, the rupee has been among the worst-performing currencies. It has depreciated from ₹63.65 to ₹68.42 and may cross ₹70.

Little Impact on Exports

During UPA I, merchandise exports tripled from USD 63 billion to USD 183 billion and, during UPA II, it grew to USD 315 billion. Under NDA, the number has remained below that peak. It touched a low of USD 262 billion in 2015–16 and struggled to close at USD 303 billion in 2017–18.

Rising Crude Oil Prices

The party that began in September 2014 is over. Crude oil prices that had plummeted to USD 26 per barrel have increased to USD 79 and threaten to rise further. Nothing was done in the last four years to increase domestic production. No major international oil company is in India in exploration except British Petroleum and Cairn—and both are reluctant to invest more in exploring new fields.

And Consequent Rise in Fuel Prices

Public anger is building against high prices of petrol and diesel. Between 2014 and 2018, due to low prices of crude oil, government saved ₹15 per litre in the cost of production of petrol and also increased the excise duty by ₹10 per litre. Same with diesel. With a relentless rise in retail prices, government has no choice but to cut the excise duties which it is loath to do. The one-trick pony has no other trick up its saddle.

Rising Inflation

After keeping inflation under control for four years, thanks to the RBI, Consumer Price Index (CPI) is poised to rise. It crossed 5 per cent in December 2017 and January 2018 and, since then, is hovering around 4.5 per cent. A good monsoon will help, a depreciating rupee will hurt.

Fall in Bond Prices, Increase in Bond Yields

Between July 2017 and May 2018, the yield has increased by 1.4 per cent and stands at 7.87 per cent. Investors in bonds, including banks, have taken a huge hit. Critics have pointed to over-borrowing by the government. The direction of bond prices and yields is not clear, sowing uncertainty in the minds of investors.

Worsening NPAs of Banks

NPAs of all scheduled banks had risen from 4.1 per cent in March 2014 to 10.2 per cent in September 2017, and have increased since. Operation Indradhanush lies in tatters. Everybody has been shot in the foot, some in the head: CEOs of banks, senior bank officials, statutory auditors, promoters and potential bidders. It will get worse.

Decline in Foreign Portfolio Investment

Net foreign portfolio investment turned negative in 2018 in February, April and May. If the US Fed were to raise interest rates, as is likely, the outflow will accelerate.

No Evidence of Job Creation

Rival claims by persons with privileged access to data and veteran analysts of the job market have only made the confusion worse. According to Labour Bureau Quarterly Surveys, only a few thousand jobs were created every quarter. If the GFCF is down from its peak by about 5 percentage points, if the average growth rate of IIP in the last four years was 4.05 per cent, and if there is no export growth, it is difficult to believe that non-farm jobs in the millions were created.

Growing Distress among Farmers, Neglect of MGNREGA

Average growth of the agriculture sector during the last four years was an anaemic 2.7 per cent. Cost +50 per cent as MSP is nowhere in sight. Most farmers do not get even the declared MSP.

MGNREGA is no longer demand-driven. Increase in the wage rate is pitiful, in many states the rate is lower than the prevailing minimum wage. 57 per cent of wage dues of workers were unpaid as of April 2018.

Disquiet over the ToR of the Fifteenth FC

It is not only the term requiring the Fifteenth FC to take into account the 2011 population Census, there are other terms that have caused concern among the states (and not only the southern states). At least seven states are firm that only amendments to the ToR will be acceptable.

As you read this, you will be submerged in the flood of propaganda that has been unleashed by the government to celebrate the completion of four years. Of course, there will be some progress under any government. If you wish to join the celebrations, do so, but remember the dire state of the economy.

GOVERNMENTS HIDE, PEOPLE SEEK

10 June 2018

On the day after the CSO released the growth numbers for 2017–18, the media played up just one number: 7.7 per cent. At first blush it appeared to be the GDP growth number for the whole year 2017–18, and was certainly impressive. Actually, it was the growth number for just one quarter, Q4, and the uptick was also because of the low base effect. For the whole year, however, the GDP growth rate was a sobering 6.7 per cent.

The government puffed up the Q4 growth rate and claimed that the worst effects of demonetisation and a flawed GST were over. Mercifully, the government stopped short of making the claim that *achche din* had arrived! At the end of four years, the government has switched over to a modest *Saaf Niyat, Sahi Vikas* (clean intention, right progress)!

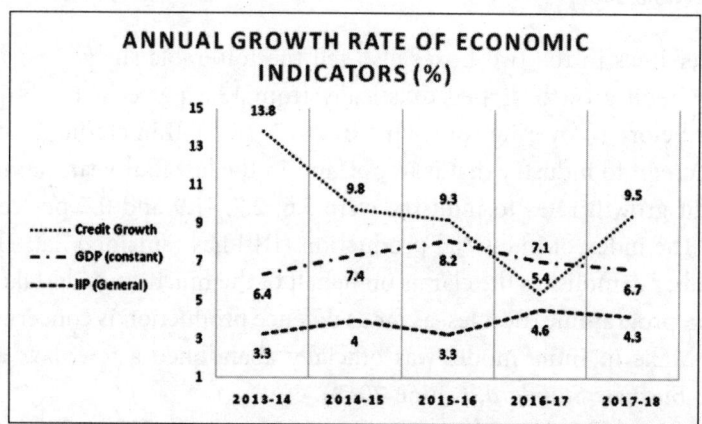

The path of the BJP-led NDA government's four-year journey is littered with too many broken promises: ₹15 lakh in every bank account, 2 crore jobs, MSP at cost + 50 per cent, waiver of agricultural loans, insurance cover to all farmers, peace and security in J&K, a good and simple GST, and many more. You can add to the list from your own experience.

Look at Outcomes

At the end of four of the five years allowed to a government, the people cannot be expected to judge a government by its intent. The correct test is outcomes. Look at the boxes with the graphs. Every line depicts a measurable parameter. And every line, after showing promise in the first year, has dipped.

Some conclusions can be drawn without fear of contradiction. Beginning 2012–13, the economy was on the mend, and the GDP growth rate accelerated from 5.5 per cent in 2012–13 to 6.4 per cent in 2013–14 to 7.4 per cent in 2014–15 to 8.2 per cent in 2016–17. The story thereafter is one of steep decline. From 8.2 per cent to 6.7 per cent in two years, it is a fall of 1.5 per cent—exactly what I had predicted after demonetisation.

Miserable Story

Other lines in the two boxes also tell the miserable story:

Credit growth dipped drastically from 13.8 per cent to 5.4 per cent before recovering somewhat in 2017–18. Within credit growth, it is credit to industry that is important. In the last four years, annual credit growth rates to industry were 5.6, 2.7, -1.9 and 0.7 per cent.

The index of industrial production (IIP) has remained flat. That number demolishes the claims on behalf of the much-touted Make in India programme. Besides, as far as defence production is concerned, the Make in India model was officially abandoned a few days ago (see *Business Standard*, 6 June 2018).

Gross NPAs have risen from ₹2,63,015 crore to ₹10,30,000 crore and will rise more. The banking system is practically bankrupt. I have not come across a banker who will willingly sanction a loan; nor an investor who will confidently borrow money. The economy is running on just one wheel—government expenditure.

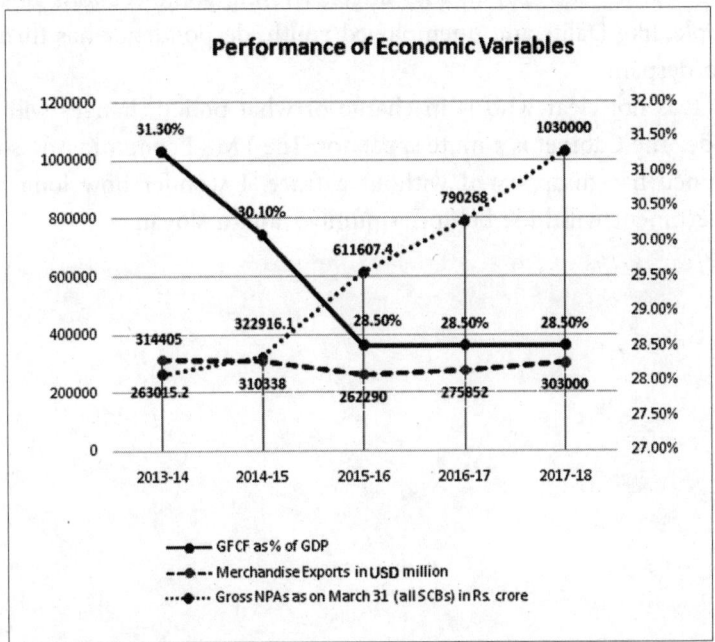

GFCF, after falling from 31.3 per cent in 2013–14 to 28.5 per cent in 2015–16, is stuck at the same level for three years, proving my point that private investment is in the doldrums.

Merchandise exports hit a peak of USD 315 billion in 2013–14. Since then, the figure has struggled to cross USD 300 billion and, in two out of the four years, it was well below USD 300 billion.

Mood of Despondency

We could pick up more economic indicators and draw the lines on a graph. It will be the same story of poor analysis and reckless decisions (demonetisation, flawed GST, stagnant farm wages, high fuel prices, intimidating tax recovery, *mala fide* investigations, etc).

The mood of the nation is despondent. In the RBI's survey (May 2018), 48 per cent of respondents felt that the economic situation had worsened in the last one year. In some sectors, like agriculture, despondency has turned into anger. Among some sections of the people, like Dalits and unemployed youth, despondency has turned into despair.

It is not clear who is in charge or what policy changes will be made. The Cabinet is a mute spectator. The PM's Economic Advisory Council has disappeared without a trace. I wonder how long the government will hide behind a number and a slogan.

CALCULATE PRICE OF A TRADE WAR

1 July 2018

It is not the Third World War, but the consequences will be serious and will hurt all countries of the world. On the trade front, the world's biggest player, the United States, has gone rogue. US President Donald Trump's policy shifts have rocked the boat of world trade that had for decades been sailing steadily away from the harbours of protectionism.

The US is arguably the most important economy from the perspective of world trade. Its share of the world's merchandise exports and imports is 9.12 per cent and 13.88 per cent, respectively. Its share of exports and imports of commercial services is 15.24 per cent and 10.27 per cent, respectively. Roughly, one-fourth of world trade in goods and services is accounted for by one country! Candidate Trump had made his intentions clear during his election campaign. Hence, the US's decision to turn protectionist is not sudden or unexpected.

Consensus Breaks Down

It is not that there was no protectionism in the trading system before the recent decisions of the US. Countries did exercise selective protectionism on select goods, especially where there were strong local interests that needed to be protected (the *swadeshi* lobbies!). However, there was a general consensus that protectionism was not a good thing and was an aberration in the general move towards open and free trade.

The US going rogue means that there is a shift in what is considered acceptable. Given how trade wars work, protectionism could soon become the norm, and decades of work on establishing a rule-based trading order may be imperilled. The recent decisions on tariffs suggest that the US President truly believes what he tweets: 'Trade wars are good and easy to win.' He is upset about China's alleged currency manipulation and by high tariffs by some countries (e.g. India's tariff on imported luxury bikes; Canada's tariff on dairy products, etc).

Contrary to Mr Trump's belief, history and experience tell us that trade wars are neither good nor easy to win. They will leave almost all countries bruised and the world as a whole will be worse off. The current trade war was triggered by the persisting imbalance in trade between the US and China (Advantage China: USD 375 billion in 2017) and is not yet a full-blown war. However, the war is drawing in other countries as well. The US and China, and the US and Europe, have raised tariffs against each other's imports. Indian exports of steel and aluminium also got caught in the crossfire just because of a USD 23 billion trade deficit for the US against India!

India Joins War

What should India's response be? India fired the first shots in December 2017 by raising tariffs on a number of products, ostensibly to boost the revenues. In the Budget for 2017–18, a desperate-for-revenue government raised tariffs on more products. In view of Mr Trump's past pronouncements, it is difficult to believe that the government's December 2017 and February 2018 steps were unrelated to, and without anticipation of, the decisions that the US government took later.

I am afraid the context has now changed. We seem to be in the middle of multiple trade wars and India has allowed itself to be dragged into the war by imposing tariffs on 28 goods from the US that will yield, if import volumes remain the same, an additional

USD 240 million. This is a huge risk for India. Growing volume of trade was one of the main drivers of the enormous expansion of world output in the post-war years. Developing countries like India could become manufacturing hubs or major service providers. Conversely, a reversal of the growth rates of trade and output will harm developing countries the most.

India's exports are quite sensitive to the volume of world trade. In the last four years, the growth rates of world trade were less-than-satisfactory; and India's merchandise export growth was negative (see Table).

Year	World Trade Growth Rate	Year	India's Merchandise Exports (USD billion)
2013	2.7	2013–14	315
2014	2.7	2014–15	310
2015	2.4	2015–16	262
2016	1.3	2016–17	276
2017	4.7	2017–18	303

Source: WTO's World Trade Statistical Reviews

Who Will Be the Loser?

A trade war and protectionism will add to a difficult economic situation. No country's economy has grown briskly (double-digit growth) without exports growing at 15 per cent or more. It is a pipe dream to grow through 'Make in India' for India. We have to 'Make in India' for the world. That means robust export growth. And this is an engine that has grossly under-performed in the last four years.

It is in India's interests to be one of the adults in the room and stand up for an open trade order. True, India is not the US or China but is big enough to count. Our share of global merchandise exports and imports is 1.65 per cent and 2.21 per cent, respectively.

Our share of exports and imports of commercial services is 3.35 per cent and 2.83 per cent, respectively. What the world requires is a coalition of sensible countries that will anchor world trade while a few countries disrupt world trade.

I offer unsolicited advice: here is an opportunity for India to avoid the path of retaliatory tariffs and negotiate with the US with the offer of more trade and lower tariffs, not less trade and higher tariffs.

DEBATE, QUESTIONS, BUT NO ANSWERS

29 July 2018

On Friday, 20 July 2018, the government reluctantly agreed to a debate on a motion of no-confidence, the first such motion in the four years and two months of the Narendra Modi government.

Numerous questions were raised by the members. Like you, I waited for the answers, especially on questions concerning the economy. What the country got by way of answers from the prime minister (in those 90-odd minutes) was more Congress-bashing, more repetition of tiresome phrases (*main kaamdar hoon*), more recitals from official handouts, and more self-congratulation (I am a partner of the poor in their sorrows, I am a partner of the youth in their dreams…)

The questions are being asked across the length and breadth of the country. Hence, I ask them in this essay (and also offer what would have been truthful answers).

Economy in a Mess

Q. In terms of economic growth, which was the worst year of the Modi government and why?

A. 2017–18, because the government has given up on reforms and gone back to the days of a *dirigiste* economy. The government seems to have discovered the virtues of control, import substitution, price control, quantitative restrictions, non-tariff barriers, retrospective taxation and punitive laws.

Q. Why are there no signs of recovery yet?

A. Because the GFCF (the investment ratio) has steeply declined from 31.3 per cent of GDP in 2013–14 and has remained stagnant in the last three years at about 28.5 per cent.

Q. How is 'Industry', especially manufacturing, doing?

A. The IIP was a low 2.6 per cent between December 2016 and October 2017. There were some signs of revival between November 2017 and February 2018. However, in March, April and May, the growth rate faltered again—4.6 per cent, 4.8 per cent, and 3.2 per cent, respectively. The slowdown is primarily in manufacturing.

Low Investment, No Jobs

Q. Did the decline in growth rate come as a surprise?

A. No, because growth depends upon credit, and growth in bank credit to industry has been about 1 per cent in most months, and sometimes even going into negative territory. The worst sufferers of credit denial are the small and medium enterprises.

Q. Why is credit growth sluggish?

A. Credit growth requires banks to be in good shape. The RBI's Financial Stability Report states that, in March 2018, the Gross Non Performing Assets ratio of banks had climbed to 11.6 per cent of their advances, up from 10.2 per cent in September 2017. The government's muddled response to the banking crisis is to simply put more taxpayers' money into the banks or to sell a nearly bankrupt bank (IDBI) to LIC.

Q. What is the position of investment?

A. In 2017–18, announcement of new investment projects declined by 38.4 per cent and completion of new projects declined by 26.8 per cent from the previous year. Foreign direct investment was also down by 15 per cent.

Many Negatives

Q. Are jobs being created?

A. No. The Centre for Monitoring Indian Economy (CMIE) reported that the number of persons employed in 2017–18 was 406.2 million—lower than the 406.7 million employed in 2016–17. The Minister of Industry, Tamil Nadu, told the state legislature that, in 2017–18, 50,000 SMEs had closed down and 500,000 jobs had been lost in his state due to demonetisation.

Q. What is the outlook on inflation?

A. Wholesale inflation in June was 5.8 per cent, the highest in more than four and a half years. The consumer price inflation was 5 per cent in June, and may rise. RBI raised the policy rate in June and may do so again in August.

Q. What has the government done to relieve agricultural distress?

A. Nothing. The Economic Survey (ES) 2018 authored by Dr Arvind Subramanian admitted that real agricultural incomes have been stagnant since 2014. The unanimous view among farmers' organisations as well as noted farm scientists and economists (such as Dr M.S. Swaminathan and Dr Ashok Gulati) is that the recent announcement of increases in MSP was a *jumla* and, absent coverage beyond paddy, wheat and cotton and absent procurement in many states, it would not benefit the majority of farmers.

Q. Is the macro-economic situation satisfactory?

A. Hardly. The CAD climbed to 1.87 per cent in 2017–18, which is the highest since 2012–13, and is poised to cross 2 per cent in 2018–19. The escalating trade wars will be a negative for India. Merchandise goods export growth has been negative in the four years and the trade balance is negative. The rupee has been in a free fall, going from ₹64.50 to a dollar on 23 June to ₹69.05 on 24 July. The government will struggle to meet the FD target of 3.3 per cent in 2018–19.

All these mean that the economy is in serious trouble and is yet to recover from the body blows dealt by the government—demonetisation, poor implementation of the GST, and tax terrorism. The BJP will get more desperate, its voice will become more shrill, the rhetoric of chest-thumping nationalism will rise, and polarisation of the electorate on religious and caste lines will be pushed harder.

There was evidence of all this in the reply given by the prime minister. The motion was lost, so was an opportunity to answer the questions of the people.

BLACK TO WHITE MAGIC

9 September 2018

Demonetisation is done but not yet dusted. With the release of the RBI's Annual Report for 2017-18, the ghost of demonetisation has come back to haunt the government of Mr Narendra Modi.

A policy may be well-intended, yet flawed. In the case of demonetisation, it is difficult to believe that the policy was well-intended because of the opaque process that was followed before the decision was announced. On 7 November 2016, the government told RBI to send its recommendation on the proposed demonetisation of currency (₹500 and ₹1,000 notes) by the next day. RBI had done no study or preparatory work; yet the Central Board of RBI hurriedly met on 8 November, without an agenda and without a background note, and dutifully 'recommended' that the notes may be declared no longer legal tender.

The Chief Economic Adviser was not consulted or taken into confidence: on 8 November he was in Kerala to deliver a talk.

A Note for Cabinet was not prepared and circulated to the Cabinet or tabled at the Cabinet meeting held on 8 November. Ministers who were present have admitted, privately, that they were 'told' at the meeting that currency will be demonetised.

Failed Objectives

Nevertheless, let me assume that the decision to demonetise currency was taken with the intention of achieving certain objectives—seizing black money, ending counterfeiting of currency notes and stopping the financing of terrorism. None of the objectives has been achieved: hoards of black (i.e. unaccounted) money in new currency notes continue to be seized; counterfeit currency in the new denominations and design continue to be detected; and terrorism continues unabated and is presumably financed by new currency notes.

In the light of the failed objectives, what should the people conclude on demonetisation? I shall reserve my conclusion for the end and look at one important outcome of demonetisation—its impact on saving, especially household saving.

More Cash, Less Saving

According to the RBI, currency in circulation on 28 October 2016 (before demonetisation) was of the value of ₹17,54,022 crore. On 17 August 2018, the currency in circulation was ₹19,17,129 crore! So, we are not a less-cash economy because of demonetisation. How is this currency in circulation accounted for? For the answer, see Table 1.

	2013–14	2015–16	2017–18
Gross Financial Saving of which	10.4	10.8	11.1
Cash	0.9	1.4	2.8
Deposits with Banks	5.8	4.6	2.9
Less Financial Liabilities	3.1	2.8	4.0
Net Financial Saving	7.2	8.1	7.1

As per cent of Gross National Disposable Income

Some facts are self-evident:

1. The people of India trust cash. They are keeping more cash with them today than in 2015–16. The amount of cash in hand has actually doubled from 1.4 to 2.8 per cent. Consequently, cash in the form of deposits with banks has declined from 4.6 to 2.9 per cent.

2. People have borrowed more and their liabilities have increased from 2.8 to 4 per cent. As a result, while the gross household saving is higher, the net household saving has declined from 8.1 to 7.1 per cent.
3. The fall in net household saving has impacted investment measured by GFCF and its components. See Table 2.

	2014–15*	2015–16*	2016–17	2017–18
GFCF	30.4	29.3	28.5†	28.5†
of which Government Investment	6.7	7.4	n.a.	n.a.
Private Investment	23.7	21.9	n.a.	n.a.

As per cent of GDP; *Economic Survey; †CSO

4. The fall in GFCF naturally affected the growth rate since demonetisation. It is too early to celebrate the 2018–19 Q1 growth rate of 8.2 per cent because it is on the lowest base of 5.6 per cent recorded in 16 quarters since the NDA came to power. Going forward, the 'base effect' will not be so favourable. Hence, even if the economy maintains its current pace of growth, the quarterly growth rate is likely to slide in the next three quarters.

Inventing Arguments

Given these facts, it is amusing to see the government's spokespersons inventing new arguments to flaunt the 'success' of demonetisation.

The favourite argument is that the tax base has increased. True, a record 5.42 crore income tax returns have been filed in the current year. But, remember that 1 crore filers return 'nil' tax liability and pay no income tax! Besides, the increase in direct tax revenue is only 6.6 per cent against a budgeted increase of 14.4 per cent.

There is also the pie-in-the-sky argument: thousands of suspicious accounts and transactions are under scrutiny. Good, but when will the process, including appeals and further appeals, be completed?

The government is counting its chicken before they are hatched. Meanwhile, the public perception is that tax terrorism has been unleashed upon individuals and businesses.

The next argument is rapid digitisation. Between 2013–14 and 2017–18, the value of digital transactions has increased annually at 14.3, 10.7, 9.1, 24.4 and 12 per cent, indicating no acceleration in the pace because of demonetisation. Moreover, digitisation has been achieved in other countries without the disruption and pain of demonetisation and could have been achieved in India too.

At the end of the day, after being told that ₹15,31,000 crore has been returned to the RBI, the general perception is that demonetisation was an ingenious device to facilitate a number of people to convert their black money into white money through a simple over-the-counter exchange at banks! Elementary, Dr Watson!

A BIG ASK IN ELECTION YEAR

16 September 2018

Numbers yo-yo up and down from month to month. Hence, economists and analysts always look for a trend, over a quarter or half year, before reaching any conclusion. After looking at data over the medium term, it appears that the foundations of macroeconomic stability of the Indian economy are becoming weaker. The trend may still be reversed and, as a concerned citizen, I hope it will be.

Let us look at the sources of the vulnerability that is causing anxiety. Firstly, the price of crude oil. Undeniably, the government reaped a bonanza in the early years. In June 2014, just after the NDA government assumed office, the price of the Indian basket of crude oil was USD 109 per barrel. From July onwards, the price started falling, reaching USD 46.6 in January 2015. From January 2015 to October 2017 (except May and June 2015), the price never crossed USD 60. Those were unbelievably low prices. This factor alone contributed hugely to improving the macroeconomic indicators. Had the prices of petrol, diesel and LPG been reduced to reflect the decline in the price of crude oil, consumers would have gained substantially. The government would have nothing of that and increased taxes on petroleum products to deprive households and businesses of the gains of lower prices. The consequence is that the government revenue has become oil-dependent, government is loath to give up easy revenues, and there is mounting anger among the people as prices of petrol, diesel and LPG soar every day.

Crude Oil Spoils Party

In my estimate (*The Indian Express*, 14 January 2016) the 'windfall' for the 12-month period (December 2014 to November 2015) was about ₹1,40,000 crore comprised of expenditure savings and additional revenue. In the two subsequent years (2016 and 2017), the 'windfall' would have been equally large. In spite of this, the government has not been able to adhere to the fiscal consolidation roadmap. In the four years of the NDA government, the FD has been 4.1, 3.9, 3.5 and 3.5 per cent and the estimate for 2018–19 is 3.3 per cent. I believe that the estimate of 3.3 per cent is based on the assumption that the price of crude oil will remain below USD 70. That seems unlikely and Brent price is close to USD 80. Hence, the first point of stress is the FD.

Secondly, exports are lower than imports every month, leaving a deficit on the trade account, but that is not unusual. However, the growth rate of exports still lags behind the growth rate of imports, and that was remediable. Nothing worthwhile was done and merchandise exports remained stagnant for four years at below USD 310 billion. The net effect is that the CAD has widened and is expected to rise from 1.87 per cent in 2017–18 to 2.5-3 per cent at the end of 2018–19. That is the second point of stress.

Thirdly, the emerging markets party seems to be over and global investors seem to be rebalancing their portfolios. As US interest rates are hardening, Foreign Portfolio Investors (FPIs) have been selling off, leading to net outflows from India. This year, the net outflows by FPIs till date, including equity, debt and hybrid, have been ₹47,891 crore. It is too early to call, but it is likely that 2018–19 will see the biggest outflow since 2008–09 (the year of the international financial crisis).

Rupee Dips, Yield Rises

Fourthly, because of these factors, the rupee is becoming weaker. Against the dollar, its conversion rate has fallen by 12.65 per cent in 2018. Four days ago, the government put out a statement that 'government and RBI will do everything to ensure that rupee does not slide to unreasonable levels.' Such assurances tend to fall flat on investors and analysts who are focused on critical numbers—FD, CAD, bond prices, return on investment net of inflation, etc—than on reassuring words. Despite the nudge to 'do everything to ensure...', the only thing that the RBI can do to arrest the depreciation is to sell dollars, but there are limits to such intervention.

Finally, in the last one year, the yield on the 10-year government bond has risen by 1.5 per cent. As I write, the yield has touched 8.13 per cent. The rate is a measure of the perceived risk of investing in India. Together with the depreciating rupee, the rate suggests that the markets are concerned about the macroeconomic stability of the country.

Don't Lose Focus

The last word may be said by the RBI in the monetary policy statement due in October. If the RBI hikes the repo rate again and changes its stance to withdrawal of accommodation, it will be because the RBI too shares the concerns about macroeconomic stability.

None of the above is unprecedented. We faced a similar situation in 1997, 2008 and 2013, albeit for different reasons. In such a situation, a small rise in the Sensex or a dip in the bond yield on a given day, or a 'steady' IIP, or a marginal fall in CPI should not be a cause for celebration. That is the yo-yo of numbers that I referred to at the beginning! Instead, the government should focus on unclogging and boosting investments, increasing bank credit (especially to industry) and keeping a tight control on expenditure. Is that a big ask?

FIVE STEPS TO NIRVANA

23 September 2018

The government has tacitly acknowledged that the economy faces a crisis. The 'crisis managers' met with the prime minister on 14 September 2018. The governor of the RBI was summoned to attend the late evening meeting. Two things were wrong about his attendance: the publicity surrounding the event and the post-meeting announcements. Why have a governor (and whither his autonomy) if the government—and no less than the finance minister—will make the announcement on measures to boost the rupee?

Be that as it may, let me focus on the five measures to 'boost the rupee'.

The objective of the five measures is to enhance the inflow of foreign currencies (up to USD 10 billion) to balance the outflow of foreign currencies and prevent the depreciation of the rupee. The catch is that foreign investments do not flow into or out of a country at the command or whim of the government of that country. They follow the command of their owners or managers who will make their own judgments about putting their money in a country.

Let me list the five measures and ask the question, will they work?

1. Mandatory hedging conditions for infrastructure loans will be reviewed

When a borrower borrows in foreign currency, he has to repay in that currency. Infrastructure loans are normally of longer tenures and the borrower does not know if, during that period, the rupee will appreciate or depreciate. So, he is advised to hedge. He will pay a small cost, but will gain if the rupee depreciated. I wonder which borrower will be foolhardy to borrow an infrastructure loan (of a long tenure) without hedging. If the rupee depreciated, will the government bear the exchange rate risk or will the RBI give the borrower dollars at the old exchange rate? Since nothing of that sort will happen, most borrowers of infrastructure loans will hedge.

2. **To permit manufacturing sector entities to avail of external commercial borrowings up to USD 50 million with a minimum maturity of one year versus the earlier period of three years**

Loans of a size under USD 50 million and a tenure of one year are akin to bridge loans or working capital loans. Borrowers will resort to such loans only if they cannot access Indian banks or the Indian market. Neither limiting the size of the loan nor allowing a shorter minimum tenure will address the question of uncertainty in the economic environment. I doubt if a lot of money will come into the country through this window.

3. **Removal of exposure limits of 20 per cent of FPI's corporate bond portfolio to a single corporate group, company and related entities, and 50 per cent of any issue of corporate bonds to be reviewed**

These limits were imposed by the RBI in April 2018 to prevent concentration of a company's or a corporate group's debt in the hands of a single FPI. Removal of the limit may help AAA-rated companies to raise more debt from a known investor. However, it will have no impact on the perception of the lender about the country's macroeconomic stability. Investors and analysts form their opinion on the basis of hard numbers—FD, CAD, central bank rate, bond yield, rate of inflation, etc.

4. Exemption from withholding tax for issuance of Masala Bond issues done in FY 2018–19 and removal of restrictions on Indian banks' market-making in Masala Bonds including restrictions on underwriting of such bonds

This is a purely temporary measure (valid until 31 March 2019) to support corporates in raising foreign loans denominated in Indian currency. If withholding tax is removed, the immediate return to the lender will be higher, but his tax liability, if any, will remain the same. It is, therefore, a small factor. In Masala Bonds, since the exchange rate risk is with the lender, the key factors are the comparative yield and the exchange rate. If those two factors are uncertain or problematic, no big change in the rate of inflows may be expected.

5. Restrictions on import of non-essential items and encouragement of exports

This is rich coming from a government that has achieved negative growth in merchandise exports in the last four years! The government no longer believes in free trade and has already taken several protectionist measures. Markets do not take kindly to such measures. Besides, promotion of exports is painstaking work, not an instant fix, and there will not be dramatic results in six months.

The rupee trade market is huge—about USD 60 billion daily in the on-shore market and an equal amount in the off-shore market. The markets' response to the five measures of the government has ranged from lukewarm to negative. Since the day of the announcement and until Friday, 21 September 2018, there has been no recovery in the exchange rate or the bond yield.

External events—rising crude oil prices, the US Treasury rate and the looming trade wars—are impacting the Indian economy. The waters are quite muddied. The government is sticking to its budget estimates (BEs) as if nothing has changed. It is unwilling to alter or calibrate its positions on the projected growth rate, government expenditure, NPA resolution, and tax enforcement. The government seems to believe that it can tide over the crisis by further muddying the muddied waters!

THINGS FALL APART; THE CENTRE CANNOT HOLD

28 October 2018

There is an old saying 'Misfortunes never come singly'. It seems that the gods are not smiling on the Indian economy.

Look at the bad news that is raining on the economy:

- Stock prices have dropped so much that the indices are trading at levels where they were 15 months ago;
- FPIs pulled out ₹35,460 crore this month until 25 October. This year, so far, the outflow has been about ₹96,000 crore. The rupee was in free fall and, among developing economies, it is one of the worst performing currencies against the US dollar. It has depreciated 16 per cent in 2018 and may fall further;
- The price of crude oil (Brent) has risen to USD 77 per barrel. Global uncertainty, especially the turmoil in the Middle East, may cause a further increase in price. The almost daily increases in the prices of petrol and diesel have imposed an intolerable burden on the consumer.

Rupee Falls, Prices Rise

- The depreciation of the rupee and the rise in prices of petroleum products have created a big hole in the pockets of consumers. Consequently, consumption of other goods and services is depressed;

- Rainfall this year has been below average. About 36 per cent of the districts have reported large deficiency in rains;
- Farmers are in revolt. The market prices of most agricultural produce are below the declared Minimum Support Prices (MSPs). Only a handful of states have procurement centres, and in insufficient numbers. So, few farmers get the MSP;
- Merchandise exports have been disappointing in the last four years and have not exceeded the level of USD 315 billion recorded in 2013–14. In the first six months of this year, it was about USD 160 billion.

Little Investment, Scarce Credit

- According to the CMIE data, new investment proposals worth only ₹1,50,000 crore were announced in July-September, 2018, well below the long-run average. CMIE data also shows that 5,394 projects are stalled.
- Growth of credit to industry has struggled to reach the level of 1.93 per cent in August 2018. In most months of the current fiscal year, the Y-O-Y growth has been barely 1 per cent.
- Non-performing assets of banks have crossed ₹10,00,000 crore. Adding to the woes of the financial sector, a systemically important NBFC, Infrastructure Leasing & Financial Services Ltd (IL&FS), has collapsed, casting a dark shadow on the entire financial sector. The insolvency cases are moving at a snail's pace, and no big case was resolved within the stipulated 180-day period.
- The employment situation is bad and likely to get worse. The CMIE has reported that the unemployment rate was 6.6 per cent in September 2018, up from 6.3 per cent in August. This is when the labour participation rate has fallen from 46+ per cent (in 2016) to 43.2 per cent.

Macro-economic Instability

- The fiscal situation is a matter of worry. Against a budgeted growth of 19.15 per cent of net tax revenue, the growth rate between April and September 2018 was only 7.45 per cent over the collection in the same period last year. To reach the budgeted number, net tax revenue has to grow by a whopping 28.21 per cent in the remaining months of the current fiscal year, which is near-impossible.
- The disinvestment programme is stalled. Against a budgeted target of ₹80,000 crore, the government has been able to raise, so far, only ₹9,686 crore. What will be the hole under this head is not yet clear.
- The Budget has assumed that public sector enterprises will give the government a dividend income of ₹1,07,312 crore this year. By being forced to absorb ₹1 per litre of petrol and diesel, the oil companies have taken a hit of ₹3,500 crore in the October-December quarter alone. Hence, their dividend distribution will be lower. The same may apply to LIC if it bails out IL&FS.
- The government is pushing programmes that are grossly underfunded. An example is the insurance-based medical care scheme, Ayushman Bharat Yojana. The goal is to cover 10 crore families (50 crore people) but the allocation, so far, is only ₹2,000 crore! Other under-funded programmes are MGNREGA, PM Awas Yojana, Drinking Water Mission, Swachh Bharat, National Health Mission and Gram Jyoti Yojana.
- The CAD at the end of September 2018 is estimated at USD 35 billion. There is no hope that it will narrow; on the contrary the year may end with a CAD of USD 80 billion or about 3 per cent of the GDP. Measures announced by the government last month were feeble and ineffective.
- The pressure on FD and CAD will push interest rates up. Bond yields have hardened. The RBI seems inclined to raise

the policy rates. If, as feared, borrowing rates go up, both investors and consumers will be hurt, depressing economic activity.

All of the above, and more, will require competent economic advisers and competent economic managers. After the exit of Dr Raghuram Rajan, Dr Arvind Panagariya and Dr Arvind Subramanian, there is no economist of international repute advising the government. Of the economic managers, the less said the better. They are busy defending the indefensible and writing blogs.

I am reminded of a line by W.B. Yeats: 'Things fall apart; the centre cannot hold.'

BUDGET

The Budget for 2018–19 was a mix of the good, bad and ugly. The numbers did not inspire confidence. Towards the end of the year, it became clear that the government was likely to miss the Budget targets of revenue and FD.

∞

COURAGE FAILS, RHETORIC REMAINS

2 February 2018

Every budget has a context, every budget must have a goal. The context of Budget 2018–19 was graphically described in the ES: the macro-economic situation was vulnerable, the exchange rate of the rupee was not competitive, real agricultural income and real agricultural wages were constant for four years, jobs were not being created, private investment had stalled and credit growth was sluggish. It was a depressing assessment. The situation called for courage, willingness to admit mistakes and take bold corrective measures. Courage was in short supply yesterday. Instead, government resorted to grand announcements.

Recall 1991 when Dr Manmohan Singh pulled India out of its cocoon of a 'closed economy' and challenged it to face the real world. Recall 1997 when a weak coalition government rewrote the tax laws of the country. Recall 2004 when the government raised its sights and aimed for double-digit growth and nearly achieved it during a period of three years. Recall 2008 when the economy overcame the challenge of an international financial crisis. Recall 2012 when the government took hard measures to put the economy back on the path of fiscal consolidation and macro stability. If one word marked those times, it was courage.

I admit that to find courage in the last year of a government's tenure is usually difficult—and especially after the Gujarat poll result and with perhaps a forewarning of the by-election results that would be announced on Budget Day. Absent courage, we have a budget without any goal and without any focus. On every test, the government's budget has failed.

- It failed the test of fiscal consolidation. The Revised Estimate (RE) of every deficit has exceeded the BE. The most glaring failure was on account of the FD—3.5 against 3.2. Even that number is doubtful. The ONGC's gift of about ₹30,000 crore—actually borrowed money—must be added to the FD. So must the ₹80,000 crore borrowed from the banks to recapitalize the banks! These numbers will not escape financial analysts and global investors;
- It failed the test of addressing unemployment. Mudra loans of average size ₹43,000 do not create jobs. A new EPFO registration does not mean a new job. Private investments create jobs, but private investment has stalled. SMEs create jobs, but many SMEs have shut down and many more have cut back production and axed jobs. Credit growth creates jobs, but with credit to 'industry' growing at 2.1 per cent it is obvious that credit is not generating new employment;
- It failed the test of addressing farm sector distress. The government took the route of squeezing prices of farm produce (inadequate MSP) in order to contain inflation. By the time it realized its mistake in the fourth year, the damage had been done. Demonetisation further damaged cash-driven agricultural production and agricultural trade. Two failed monsoons added to the woes of the farm sector. Offering, at this stage, to fix MSP at 1.5 times the cost is welcome but does not carry credibility. Nor will it bring relief until after the next kharif and rabi seasons. Farmers are angry and are showing their anger at the polling stations;
- It failed the test of promoting welfare. The ES confessed that the three challenges that the government had not addressed adequately in the last four years were agriculture, employment and education. Under education, the ES clubbed both education and healthcare. The Annual Status of Education Report (ASER)

and National Achievement Survey are a severe indictment of the central and state governments on education. The National Family Health Survey 2015–16 is an indictment on healthcare. The budget has announced the 'world's largest government funded healthcare programme'. Is it for real? It appears to be an insurance scheme, but no scheme has been designed or approved so far. More importantly, I did not find any outlay or allocation for the scheme. Will it be implemented in 2018–19? Of course not. It is an announcement, a *jumla*. The budget has also slashed the outlays on many critical schemes such as Pradhan Mantri Awas Yojana, National Drinking Water Mission, Swachh Bharat Mission, National Health Mission, Gram Jyoti Yojana, etc.

It is clear the government has run out of ideas. Mercifully, the budget did not coin new slogans or invent new acronyms. Government hopes that rhetoric will be the wind that fills its sails. The truth is that the people are tired of slogans, acronyms and rhetoric.

GOOD DOCTOR, BAD PATIENT

4 February 2018

There is an unusual, but time-honoured, arrangement in the Ministry of Finance (MoF). Apart from the many secretaries to the government, there is the post of Chief Economic Adviser (CEA). He is an employee of the government (MoF), but he is also, in a sense, independent of the government. He can hold and express (in restrained language) views contrary to the government's views. He can criticize (in polite words) policies and programmes of the government. He has a lot of freedom in preparing and presenting the ES and advising the government—a freedom not available to other secretaries to the government. The government, of course, has the freedom to reject his advice.

I regarded the CEA as the doctor-in-residence to check his patient's health every day and, in case the patient fell ill, to prescribe the course of treatment and the medicines. A bad patient will not take the medicines and make his own diagnosis and prescription.

Economic Survey vs Budget

Dr Arvind Subramanian has been a good doctor since his appointment as the CEA in October 2014. The NDA government has been a terrible patient. The uneasy relationship between a good doctor and a bad patient is best illustrated by the divergence between the ES and the Budget.

Let me illustrate:

1. The ES emphasized the four 'R's (Recognition, Resolution, Recapitalization and Reforms) and pointed out that, although the first three had been done, banking reforms had not been undertaken. The Budget was the occasion to outline the reforms and set a schedule. Instead, what we got was Elizabethan prose about 'an ambitious reform agenda under the rubric of an EASE programme'. It was another case of the tail (acronym) wagging the dog (programme).
2. The ES defined strategic disinvestment as 'adopting a pragmatic approach for the government to exit from non-strategic business to optimize economic potential for business enterprises by promoting efficiency and professional management in the company.' The government declared the government's prize strategic investment was collecting ₹37,000 crore from ONGC! The oil exploration company borrowed the money to pay government for HPCL's shares that will reduce the FD by 0.2 per cent. It was a stratagem, not a strategy.
3. The ES doctor had a medley of drugs to boost exports. The patient dismissed the concerns in one sentence and pronounced that he was hale and hearty: 'Our exports are expected to grow at 15 per cent in 2017–18.' Not a word more. A modest rise in exports in recent months may have made the government complacent. There are no grounds for complacency because merchandise exports have barely come back to the level of a few years ago. Besides, the finance minister was wrong. Export growth during April–December 2017 over the same period last year was 11.24 per cent and not 15 per cent.

Aggressive Tax Estimates

4. On tax revenues, the ES pointed out that 'It is striking that the Centre's tax-GDP ratio is no higher than it was in the 1980s' and observed, after demonetisation and the GST, it would be interesting to see how good the collections have been and also the projections for the next year. Based on REs, it appears that

the gross tax to GDP ratio will be 11.6 per cent in 2017–18. Nevertheless, the government has predicted that in 2018–19, income-tax will grow at 19.8 per cent, the GST will grow at a whopping 67 per cent and gross tax revenue will grow at 16.7 per cent. Notwithstanding the doctor's concerns, a very ill person has left an aggressive will.

5. The ES identified the headwinds to growth: the backlash against globalization, the difficulties of transferring resources from low-productivity to high-productivity sectors, the challenge of upgrading human capital to the demands of a technology-intensive workplace, and coping with climate change-induced agricultural stress. The government abandoned Planet Earth and soared into space to declare 'Combining cyber and physical systems have great potential to transform not only innovation ecosystem but also our economies and the way we live. To invest in research, training and skilling in robotics, artificial intelligence, digital manufacturing, big data analysis, quantum communication and internet of things…will launch a Mission on Cyber Physical Systems to support establishment of centres of excellence.' I suppose we must wait for the finance minister to return from his space odyssey to remind him of the headwinds on Earth.

6. The ES pointed out that savings and private investments had been consistently falling for a few years, that the twin engines that propelled the economy's take-off in the mid-2000s are running below take-off speed, and the government must announce a roadmap for reviving private investments. In the Budget, the finance minister did not even acknowledge the worrying situation of savings and investments!

Paying Lip Service

7. The ES highlighted the importance of health and education for maintaining competitiveness. The finance minister spoke extensively on the two issues, but this is what he did when it came to allocating funds:

	2017-18 RE	(₹crore) 2018-19 BE
Expenditure		
Education	81,869	85,010
Health	53,198	54,667
Outlay		
National Health Mission	31,292	30,634
National Education Mission	29,556	32,613

The government continues to be in denial. It denies the objective situation in the economy. It denies farm distress. It denies joblessness. It denies the arguments of the Opposition. Now, it denies even the diagnosis and the prescription of the doctor it engaged in 2014.

MORE VOICES AGAINST BUDGET PROVISIONS

18 February 2018

February 2018 taught me—and I hope many others—a lesson in politics: that 25 years are long enough to erase memories of the past, especially the economic past. Twenty-seven years ago, India was a closed economy.

- Imports were bad, import substitution was good;
- Tariffs were good, higher tariffs meant safer economy;
- Foreign exchange was a precious commodity, so we hoarded what little we had;
- Taxes were necessary, higher taxes underlined dire necessity;
- High-interest rates benefit depositors and bankers, borrowers and investors be damned.

It did not matter that India was a poor country and the Indian people—the overwhelming majority—were poor. At least they were safe, or so we believed. And then happened two unlikely events. A cruel accident of history placed P.V. Narasimha Rao in the office of the Prime Minister of India. And he appointed an unassuming scholar, Dr Manmohan Singh, as Finance Minister. Both had been long-serving, loyal members of the Establishment and were expected to defend the Establishment.

Deconstructing the Hard Work

On 3 July 1991, India woke up to the fact that a demolition squad had assumed power in New Delhi. Brick by brick, the old structure was brought down; brick by brick, a new edifice was erected. After 27 years, it is still work-in-progress.

Unfortunately, another demolition squad seems to have insidiously burrowed its way to the seat of power in New Delhi. This squad seems to have begun the work of deconstructing the edifice that was painstakingly built over the last 27 years and re-erecting the *dirigiste* economy that was the cause of India's long history of low growth. How else can one explain the recent decisions, including the ones that were part of the Budget speech?

Since 1991, India's 'Manufacturing' sector has grown at about the same average rate as the GDP/GVA. However, exports have increased. Exports in 1990–91 amounted to 6.93 per cent of GDP. By 2016–17, the proportion had increased to 19.31 per cent. It is wrong to assume that the manufacturing sector will grow, or that exports will increase, only behind protectionist walls. On the contrary, protectionism will starve the country of capital and technology and will make the manufacturing sector's exports uncompetitive.

There are enough safeguards against unfair trade practices. The WTO agreements allow a country to impose tariffs subject to ceilings. 'Surge' in imports can be countered by imposing Safeguard duties for a temporary period. 'Dumping' can be penalized by imposing Anti-dumping duties. Besides, there are permissible non-tariff measures to prevent cheap, poor quality goods invading the Indian market. Major manufacturing and trading countries have prospered under an open, competitive and rule-based world trade system. India too has benefited.

Reversing the Direction

Is there a re-think under pressure from the so-called *swadeshi* lobbies? Just before the budget, and in the budget, the government announced a number of measures that seemed to suggest that the protectionist (and taxation) lobbies have gained strength. Here are some of them:

1. In December 2017, Customs duties were increased significantly on a number of electric and electronic items such as mobile telephones (0–15 per cent), microwave ovens, cameras, monitors, etc. Apparently, this was not a short-term measure.
2. Huge increases in tariff were announced in the budget on a large number of goods, including fruit juices, perfumes and toiletry products, automobile parts, footwear, imitation jewellery, mobile telephones (20 per cent), smart watches, toys and games, silk fabrics, vegetable oils, and a number of miscellaneous items like kites, candles, sunglasses, etc.
3. Capital is being taxed in multiple ways. The RBI has identified five taxes on capital, including the latest Long Term Capital Gains (LTCG) tax, which will inhibit investment.
4. National Stock Exchange and Bombay Stock Exchange have terminated their licence agreements with the Singapore Stock Exchange on sharing live data, ostensibly to prevent the index futures market from shifting to Singapore to benefit from less taxes and lighter regulation.
5. The FD will be allowed to rise this year and next year above the targets announced earlier, unmindful of the impact on inflation which, according to the RBI, may increase to 5.6 per cent during April–September 2018.
6. Every rise in crude oil prices will be reflected in the retail prices of petrol, diesel and LPG, with no thought given to the alternative of cutting excise duties on these petroleum products or bringing them under the GST.

Confession of Failure

Taking protectionist measures is a confession that the Make in India campaign has flopped, that the much-trumpeted rise in the index of Ease of Doing Business is an illusion, and the claim of improved infrastructure is an empty boast. Voices of dissent are now being heard from within the Establishment.

Dr Arvind Panagariya, former vice-chairman, NITI Aayog, has been scathing on the increase in Customs duties. Dr Rathin Roy, Member, Prime Minister's Economic Advisory Council (PMEAC), has criticized the breach of FD targets. Dr Surjit Bhalla, another Member, PMEAC, has lambasted the LTCG. Dr Rajiv Kumar, vice chairman, NITI Aayog, has lamely expressed the hope that the measures will be temporary.

The Monetary Policy Committee of the RBI has listed six uncertainties that will be inflationary. Three of them are directly related to the budget announcements. I am reminded of what George Santayana said: 'Those who do not remember the past are condemned to repeat it.'

THE HOLE IN THE BUDGET

11 March 2018

When the numbers are finally put in the left or right column and a balance is struck, the government's budget statement does not look much different from a homemaker's household budget. If we ignore the zeros, it could be the annual household budget of a rich family.

The deficit is ₹6,24,276 crore. In the case of a homemaker, there is no option but to borrow the money, if he or she has the capacity to borrow and someone is willing to lend. In the case of the government, the option is the same—to borrow—but the conditions are different.

Take a look at the numbers of India's annual budget for 2018–19:

Total Receipts	*Total Expenditure*
18,17,937	24,42,213
	(in ₹crore)

A government will borrow, whether it has the capacity to borrow or not. Some governments borrow beyond their capacity and leave a huge debt for the succeeding government.

A government may borrow in the hope that the borrowing will be temporary and the 'excess' borrowing can be set off by finding additional receipts within the year.

Behind the Numbers

According to Budget 2018-19, the central government will borrow ₹6,24,276 crore. This is the famous FD. As in the case of all numbers, the true story is not visible by just looking at the numbers. One must go behind the numbers and that is what I propose to do in this essay.

First, let's look at the receipts. The bulk of the receipts is made up of tax revenue (net to the central government). The major heads of taxes and what they are expected to fetch are in the following table.

	(Gross Collections in ₹crore)
Corporation Tax	6,21,000
Income Tax	5,29,000
Customs	1,12,500
Excise	2,59,600
GST	7,43,900
CGST	6,03,900
IGST	50,000
Cess	90,000

The elephant in the room is the GST. The GST was introduced on 1 July 2017. As per data published by the Controller General of Accounts (CGA), in the period August 2017 to January 2018, CGST collections (including IGST settlement) averaged ₹22,129 crore per month. The budget assumes that the average collection will rise to ₹44,314 crore in February and March 2018, and then increase to ₹50,000 crore per month in 2018-19. This strains credulity.

On a generous assumption that CGST collections will increase to ₹40,000 crore per month, and an annual collection of ₹4,80,000 crore, there will be a shortfall of ₹1,23,900 crore (gross) and of ₹71,862 crore (net to the Centre at 58 per cent).

The other question mark on the Receipts side is Disinvestment Receipts. In 2017-18, the BE was ₹72,500 crore but the RE is ₹1,00,000 crore. This was achieved by a sleight of hand: asking ONGC to buy the government's shareholding in HPCL and pocketing ₹36,915 crore. Can it be repeated in 2018–19? If that is not possible, the BE of Disinvestment Receipts in an election year of ₹80,000 crore (more than the BE of 2017–18) appears difficult to achieve. Hence, there could be a hole under this head too of, say, about ₹20,000 crore.

Understated Expenditure

Let's look at the expenditure side. There are two gaping holes.

Firstly, the provision for food subsidy. In 2016–17, it was about ₹1,10,000 crore, and in 2017–18 the estimate is about ₹1,40,000 crore. The provision for 2018–19 is about ₹1,70,000 crore. The increase of ₹30,000 crore in 2018–19 may not be sufficient. The NDA government was quite miserly in granting MSP. Considering it is the election year, the government made a grand announcement of giving MSP at 'cost plus 50 per cent'. It is still not clear how the 'cost' will be reckoned. But if the government were to announce large increases in MSP, the provision of ₹1,70,000 crore will not be sufficient.

Secondly, the National Health Protection Scheme is entirely unfunded. If it is a *jumla* (akin to the announcement in Budget 2016–17), there is nothing to worry. But if the government rolls out the scheme in 2018–19 and buys insurance for the beneficiaries, it has to spend money. Estimates vary from an optimistic ₹11,000 crore to a realistic ₹1,00,000 crore. That number has to be added on the Expenditure side. Under these two heads, my guess is that the government will be required to spend another ₹70,000 crore–₹20,000 crore for food subsidy and ₹50,000 crore for health insurance.

How Big Is the Hole?

I have not taken into account any rise in crude oil prices. The budget seems to have assumed that crude oil price will remain below USD 70 per barrel. If that number goes up, there will be serious trouble. When we add these numbers on both sides of the statement of account, we will have a shortfall of about ₹92,000 crore on the Receipts side and additional outgo of ₹70,000 crore on the Expenditure side—that is an addition of ₹1,62,000 to the FD.

The FD in 2018–19 is, therefore, not likely to be contained at ₹6,24,276 crore or 3.3 per cent of GDP. It may rise to ₹7,86,276 crore or 4.15 per cent of GDP. The markets are watching. You should be too, because the borrowing is your debt.

POLITICS

The big change in 2018 was in the political arena. From being virtually unchallenged, the BJP faced stiff opposition in many states from a number of political parties. The loss in the election in Karnataka was a warning bell to the BJP. The defeat of the BJP in Chhattisgarh, Madhya Pradesh and Rajasthan was a hard blow and immediately galvanized the Congress and other Opposition parties. At the end of the year, it seemed that the BJP and the Opposition had drawn level with the Opposition parties enjoying an edge in many states.

A MESSAGE LOUD AND CLEAR

18 March 2018

Two apparently unconnected events happened on Wednesday, 14 March 2018. All demands for grants were 'guillotined' (i.e. moneys were allocated without a debate) and the Lok Sabha passed the Finance Bill 2018 without a discussion. Three Lok Sabha constituencies in Uttar Pradesh and Bihar voted decisively in favour of the candidate who defeated the BJP's candidate. The first event represented the arrogance of a party's power, the second the assertion of people's power.

I am fascinated by events and incidents that illustrate the fact that, more than any person or institution, it is the people of India who will call the government's callousness, ineptitude and bluff. From Maharashtra to Gujarat to Rajasthan to Uttar Pradesh to Bihar, the gathering storm is plainly evident. Rural India is in acute distress and urban India is divided among the helpless poor and the middle class and the palanquin-bearing sections that will go along with any regime.

Agriculture in Crisis

Let's begin with rural India. 60 per cent of the population is dependent—as its main source of livelihood—on agriculture (whose share in GDP is just 16 per cent). They include small farmers, landless agricultural labourers, family labour, village industries, vendors in the village markets, petty shopkeepers, and the small service providers.

They are the poor. Their poverty affects every aspect of their lives—from their children's education to access to healthcare to finding meaningful employment. When agriculture is affected, the lives of 60 per cent of the population are affected. When agricultural income falls, those who earn non-agricultural income also see a fall in their income.

What is the record of the NDA government in the last four years? The ES 2017–18 said: 'The level of real agricultural GDP and real agricultural incomes has remained constant.' That conclusion alone captures the state of agriculture after four years of the NDA government.

Why did this happen? For four years, the NDA government kept the increase in MSP to a bare minimum. Gross Capital Formation (GCF) in agriculture fell from 2.9 per cent of GDP in 2013–14 to 2.17 per cent in 2016–17. In 2016–17, there was a good monsoon, but just when farmers were taking their produce to the market, demonetisation dealt a body blow and prices of agricultural products crashed. The search of rural youth for non-farm jobs was futile because demonetisation and a flawed GST destroyed millions of jobs in the small and medium business sector.

Is there any wonder that over 30,000 farmers marched 170 km in Maharashtra to voice their protest? Their demands were not unusual or extraordinary: they included farm loan waiver, remunerative prices, no land acquisition without consent, vesting of temple lands and pasture lands in the tillers, increase in pension to poor farmers and farm labourers, compensation for loss due to hailstorm or pest attacks, and conferring rights under the Forest Rights Act. Neither Parliament nor the state legislatures seem able or willing to listen to the farmers' woes and act. Farmers' protests will intensify across Rajasthan, Haryana, Uttar Pradesh, Madhya Pradesh, Chhattisgarh and Jharkhand.

The By-election Surprise

Gorakhpur and Phulpur (in Uttar Pradesh)—one largely rural, the other mainly urban—tell another story. Gorakhpur was an authoritarian enclave in a so-called democratic state. The moral police (Hindu Yuva Vahini) was born there. Under the BJP government, the state has brazenly defended its bias towards one religion and the 'right' of the state to kill suspected criminals in encounters that are obviously staged. The government has little to show by way of development or jobs. The voters—especially the Dalits, the Other Backward Classes, the minorities and the unemployed youth—have revolted.

Araria (in Bihar) was another kind of revolt. It was a revolt against the moral mask of anti-corruption warriors worn by the rulers to hide their ineptitude, crass opportunism and failure to deliver on the promise of 'double-engine growth'.

The passage of the Finance Bill (which is a Money Bill) without a discussion is another blow to democracy. It is the responsibility of the Treasury benches to run the House and transact government business. Brushing aside the responsibility, and emboldened by the absolute majority enjoyed in the Lok Sabha, the government has looked upon the Opposition benches with contempt, especially in passing Bills in the Lok Sabha. It is only in the Rajya Sabha that the government has shown some respect to the Opposition, but even that minimum respect has been denied with a Money Bill, where the Rajya Sabha can do nothing.

People's Vigil

The people are watching. There is no more talk of *achche din*. Every promise—₹15 lakh deposit, two crore jobs per year, doubling farmers' incomes, double-digit growth, permanent solution to the Kashmir issue, and teaching Pakistan a final lesson—has turned out to be hollow and the people know that.

The people also know that, in the present circumstances, there is not a sole political party that can displace the BJP. Hence, they are voting for the candidate who can defeat the BJP's candidate. The people are looking for a strong alternative narrative. An alternative narrative can be built on debt forgiveness, remunerative prices for farm products, generous credit, revival of small and medium businesses, a stable and rewarding business environment for the private sector, creation of jobs, and safety nets for the poor and vulnerable sections of the people. The message sent by the average voter is loud and clear. It must be heard by the Opposition parties, including the Congress.

CHANGE BEGINS WITH WORDS AND IDEAS

25 March 2018

Measuring growth is a problem. It is a bigger problem if you change the rules in the middle of the game.

GDP is the gross domestic product. Keeping aside the nuances, it is the gross value of the country's output of goods and services in a financial year. The output is valued in current prices as well as in constant prices (the latter are prices adjusted for inflation). In order to value the output at constant prices, the statistician takes a 'Base Year'.

Beginning 2004–05, the first year of the UPA government, the GDP was computed using 1999–2000 as the base year. After a few years, the base year was changed to 2004–05 but the methodology remained the same.

Serious Misgivings

What the BJP government did in 2014–15 was to change the *base year* to 2011–12 as well as change the *methodology*. I shall not go into the details of the changes; suffice to say that when the CSO reports a growth rate of 7.5 per cent in constant prices, many economists and analysts believe that it is perhaps equal to 5.5 per cent under the UPA government. There is a simple way to put an end to the misgivings: the CSO should publish the growth rates from 2004–05 computed under the old and the new methodologies, so that people and users of the data can draw their own conclusions. For reasons that are inexplicable, the government and the CSO have stubbornly refused to do so. Hence, the doubts persist.

Be that as it may, one doesn't get the feeling that the economy is growing at 7.5 per cent or thereabouts because other data point in the opposite direction. The average growth rate of the agriculture sector in the last four years has been an anaemic 2.7 per cent (compared to 4 per cent in the 10 years of the UPA), and farmers are in acute distress. The ES candidly admitted that 'real agricultural GDP and real agricultural revenues have stagnated in the last four years'. Merchandise exports in each of the last four years did not cross the level of USD 315 billion achieved in 2013–14. GFCF in current prices has steadily declined from 31.3 per cent in 2013–14 to 30.08, 28.47, 28.53 and 28.49 per cent in the last four years.

Alternative Narrative

At the ground level, the sense is of an economy growing at a low rate because there is growing unemployment and no new jobs. Dr Raghuram Rajan said a few days ago that an economy growing at 7.5 per cent will not create the jobs that are needed and called for pushing the growth rate to 10 per cent. The unstated premise is that the economy is not growing at the '7.5 per cent' rate of the earlier years when other indicators also pointed in the same direction and a significant number of jobs was created; the current '7.5 per cent' rate does not create jobs, and hence the rate itself is seriously questionable.

I don't expect anything more from this government in the next 12 months. The people have to look beyond the present government and to an alternative narrative. At the AICC Plenary Session last weekend, the Congress summed up the difference in economic philosophies: 'The Congress Party believes in the goals of inclusive economic growth through private enterprise and a competitive and viable public sector and a robust social safety net through a strong welfare state. The BJP believes in a coercive economic regime that favours a few, trickle-down growth for the middle class, and leaving the very poor to fend for themselves.'

New Ideas, New Emphasis

Some seeds that were sown earlier sprouted at the AICC Plenary Session last weekend. I wish to draw attention to a few statements of intent.

- The Congress reaffirms its conviction that the State has to play a critical role in ensuring that every Indian receives high quality primary education and healthcare;
- Good, productive jobs can be created in large numbers by India's private sector driven by trade, manufacturing, construction and exports;
- The Congress resolves to win back economic freedom for India's entrepreneurs, especially the micro, small and medium business persons, protect them from harassment and provide a stable business environment.

Among the challenges identified were:

- Generating productive jobs for millions of youth;
- Restoring robust credit growth, promoting new investments and reviving manufacturing to produce on the scale and quality demanded by the domestic and world markets.

And the Congress party's economic policy doctrine will rest on tenets including:

- Large investments by the State in education, healthcare and social safety nets, and an efficient public service delivery system;
- A conducive social and policy climate to foster business confidence, reward risk-taking and promote employment with security.

Many of the words may be familiar, but the emphasis is different. There are also new words and phrases that could flower into a new narrative. India's **private sector** finds a prominent mention; creating **good, productive jobs** is the objective; **trade, manufacturing,**

construction and exports are identified as the leading sectors; winning back **economic freedom** for India's entrepreneurs is a promise; banishing fear of economic oppression, **tax terrorism and overbearing regulation** is a goal; and fostering business confidence and **rewarding risk-taking** will be the policy.

I believe that change begins with words and ideas.

STATE ELECTION, NATION-WIDE EFFECT

6 May 2018

Thanks to the media, 'Karnataka goes to polls' sounds or reads like 'India goes to war'. Characteristically, Mr Narendra Modi will address 15 rallies in five days. No prime minister before has pushed himself/herself to the frontline of election battles in states as Mr Modi has done.

It is the strategy of a high-stakes gambler. The strategy paid huge dividends in Uttar Pradesh where the BJP was the challenger to the incumbent party (Samajwadi Party) and to the previous incumbent party (Bahujan Samaj Party [BSP]). That Mr Modi had been elected to the Lok Sabha from Varanasi, that he spoke Hindi, and that his party was able to provoke communal conflicts were helpful factors.

Karnataka not Gujarat

The strategy came perilously close to failure in Gujarat. Mr Modi's last-hour plea to save the honour of a fellow Gujarati bailed his party out and the BJP limped past the finish line with a slim majority of seven seats. The strategy is being tried again in Karnataka.

In Gujarat, the BJP and its government controlled the election narrative, in Karnataka the Congress and its government do. In Gujarat, Mr Modi was the 'native son', in Karnataka Mr Siddaramaiah is. In Gujarat, Mr Modi spoke in Gujarati, in Karnataka Mr Modi is constrained to speak through a translator. In Gujarat, the face of the BJP that sought another term was Mr Modi (and no one was projected as the next chief minister), in Karnataka the face of the BJP is Mr Yeddyurappa. In Gujarat, the BJP was able to polarise a section of the population, in Karnataka its attempts on this behalf (e.g. in south Karnataka) have failed so far.

Smart Governance

The Congress government in Karnataka was formed in May 2013. The Gross State Domestic Product (GSDP) in constant prices was ₹6,43,292 crore in 2012–13. It increased to ₹9,49,111 crore in 2017–18. Real GSDP growth was over 8 per cent a year. The average resident of Karnataka is richer: per capita income, in current prices, jumped from ₹77,309 to ₹1,74,551 during the same period, a growth of over 125 per cent. In comparison, the per capita income of the whole country increased by about 59 per cent. Unemployment (April 2018) in Karnataka is among the lowest for all the states at 2.6 per cent (Gujarat 5.0, India 5.9).

Mr Siddaramaiah has been able to push growth by keeping the tax to GSDP ratio practically constant (average of 9.5 per cent) and using the FD limit of 3 per cent to borrow more and invest and spend more. During the five years, the average FD was 2.26 per cent and the average revenue surplus was 0.08 per cent. Social sector expenditure has been consistently over 40 per cent of total expenditure. The benefits are visible, for example, in the fall in infant mortality rate, increase in electricity consumption, and rise in the number of new projects announced.

Mr Siddaramaiah has also played his political cards cleverly. By calling the JD(S) the B-team of the BJP, he has split the Opposition votes. The label has stuck to Mr Kumaraswamy. By stressing on the use of Kannada language (and opposing the use of Hindi), he has blunted the effect of the oratory of Mr Modi. Every Hindi speech of Mr Modi is viewed by a section of the people as imposition of Hindi! By supporting the demand to recognise the Lingayats as a minority, he has split a reliable vote bank of the BJP. Every Lingayat vote that shifts from the BJP to the Congress has a value of two!

Will Karnataka Push Back?

There are still six days to polling.[1] The Congress government must maintain communal harmony and peace in those crucial days. The Election Commission (EC) must not feign helplessness in curbing the distribution of money (as it did in Tamil Nadu in 2016). Mr Siddaramaiah must prove that his decision to contest from two seats did not prevent him from campaigning vigorously for the maximum number of Congress candidates. Above all, he must keep the focus on 2 Reddys + 1 Yeddy—a slogan gifted by Mr Modi!

This time the BJP is not boasting of a victory. It is placing its bet on preventing an absolute majority for the Congress and joining hands with the JD(S) to form the government. For the BJP, that is a paid for and proven formula (Manipur, Goa, Meghalaya)!

Karnataka is a great opportunity for the voters who are concerned about the slide in the governance of the country. Among them are the Dalits, the minorities, women, and the liberal and secular, but proud, Hindus. Among them are those who were worst affected by demonetisation and those who continue to be affected by a flawed GST. Among them are the first-time voters of 2014 who were lured by the promise of jobs and were thoroughly disillusioned when told to 'go and fry pakoras'. Will they push back against a growing political culture of ignorance, intolerance, bigotry and violence, and the willingness of the BJP's leadership to 'normalise' such behaviour? Intuitively, I think those voters constitute the majority, but that will be known only on 15 May 2018.

The stakes are low for the JD(S), high for the Congress, and highest for the BJP. Whatever be the result, it will cast a long shadow until May 2019.

---

[1] Polling was on 12 May 2018

WHO WILL SAVE THE CONSTITUTION?

20 May 2018

Let me remind myself—before others remind me—of what I wrote on 19 March 2017. Elections had been concluded in Uttar Pradesh, Uttarakhand, Punjab, Goa and Manipur. The BJP won in Uttar Pradesh and Uttarakhand, the Congress won in Punjab. Referring to the other two states, I wrote: 'In Goa and Manipur, the loser stole the election.' I based my remark on the following: 'The party that secured the highest number of seats would be invited first to form the government... By that rule or convention, the Congress should have been invited to form the government in Goa (17/40 seats) and in Manipur (28/60).' The controversy was around the principles to be followed by a governor in inviting a person to form the government. In the absence of a party that had secured an absolute majority, should the governor invite the single largest party or a post-poll alliance (that *prima facie* had the majority)?

The Last Statement of Law

The question had been examined in the past and there were observations in several judgments. Goa presented a concrete opportunity. In an order dated 14 March 2017, and made in Chandrakant Kavlekar vs. Union of India, the Supreme Court observed: 'The (Goa) Assembly comprises of 40 elected members. The party having the support of at least 21 elected members would obviously have majority. Annexure-B reveals that besides the 13 elected members from the BJP Legislative Party, 3 members from the Maharashtrawadi Gomantak Party, Goa, and another 3 members from the Goa Forward Party have expressed their support to the BJP Legislature Party. Besides the above, two elected independent members have also been mentioned in the letter of the governor—Annexure B—as having expressed their allegiance to the BJP Legislature Party. It is, therefore, that the BJP Legislature Party is shown to have the support of 21 MLAs.' The Supreme Court upheld the governor's decision and allowed Mr Manohar Parrikar (who had not contested the election) to prove his majority—but directed him to do so in two days, by 16 March 2017. So, I was wrong on the law. Mr Arun Jaitley's view, stated in his famous blog, was held to be right.

Governor Mocks at Court

The Goa verdict is the law declared by the Supreme Court under Article 141 of the Constitution. Under Article 144, all authorities are bound to act in aid of the Supreme Court. Goa was a text book case that the governor of Karnataka ought to have followed. It was the last and latest pronouncement on the subject by the Supreme Court. That Governor Vajubhai Vala did not will remain a blot on his record. He was loyal to the RSS/BJP and not to the Constitution of India. Once the orders were given from the top, events unfolded rapidly in Karnataka. A letter inviting Mr Yeddyurappa to form the government and prove his majority within 15 days was delivered late in the evening on 16 May, the Congress and JD(S) moved the Supreme Court just before midnight on that day, a post-midnight hearing was granted by a three-member Bench, notice and certain interim directions were issued but there was no stay of the swearing-in, and Mr Yeddyurappa was sworn in as chief minister on 17 May. The case before the Supreme Court was heard on 18 May 2018.

Saving the Constitution

The hearing, and the directions, were a blow to the designs of the BJP. The Supreme Court's order can be faulted on only one ground: after having demanded and got the letter(s) written by Mr Yeddyurappa to the governor staking his claim, the Supreme Court must have noticed that Mr Yeddyurappa had never claimed that he enjoyed the support of the majority of the elected legislators! The governor's invitation to him also did not mention any number! On this ground alone, the Supreme Court would have been justified in quashing the appointment of Mr Yeddyurappa as chief minister and directing the governor to take a fresh decision, but the Court was kind to both. Everything else in the order of the Court dated 18 May was unexceptionable:

- Take the vote of confidence on 19 May at 4 pm;
- Vote not by secret ballot;
- No appointment of an Anglo Indian member for the present;
- No major administrative decision until Mr Yeddyurappa secured a vote of confidence.

I salute the Supreme Court. The Court has done its utmost to save the Constitution from being ravaged by a group of power-hungry people. The question that remains—as I send this essay to the newspapers—is, will the legislators elected on their respective party symbols remain faithful to the party, to the voters who supported them, to the unwritten rules of a democracy, and to the Constitution of India?

Postscript: Thanks to the Supreme Court, every citizen watching the proceedings of the Karnataka Assembly live became a *pro tem* Speaker. After covering themselves with everlasting shame, before the vote could be taken, the leaders of the BJP threw in the towel. The 75-year-old pretender resigned. The puppeteers went into hiding. Democracy in Karnataka has been saved—for the time being.

MR A.B. VAJPAYEE, RIP

19 August 2018

Mr Atal Bihari Vajpayee, 93, passed away last Thursday after a long battle with illness. He started his political career as a *swayamsevak*, remained a member of the Jana Sangh until its merger in the Janata Party, founded the BJP with Mr L.K. Advani in 1980, and remained loyal to his party until his last day.

To most of his party colleagues and the RSS, he was the right man to lead the 'right' party. To many belonging to other parties, he was the right man in the wrong party!

I saw Vajpayeeji from a respectful distance. When I entered Parliament in 1984, he had lost the election to the Lok Sabha and subsequently became a member of the Rajya Sabha. The Bofors deal provided a lifeline to many parties that had been decimated in the previous election, and none gained more than the BJP. However, the unlikely winner was V.P. Singh. Between 1989 and 1991, Vajpayeeji and I sat on the Opposition benches, the difference being that his party supported the V.P. Singh government while my party opposed it. It came as no surprise that the contradictions between a Congressman-turned-anti-Congressman (V.P. Singh) and the BJP erupted in 11 months—leading to the jibe that it was Mandal vs Kamandal.

Reassuring Face of BJP

For the next six years, Indian politics was marked by a bitter struggle for primacy between a weakened Congress and a resurgent BJP. The driving force was Mr L.K. Advani, the reassuring face was Vajpayeeji.

Atal Bihari Vajpayee took oath as Prime Minister thrice. His first government—a gross miscalculation—lasted all of 13 days. His second government huffed and puffed and ultimately fell in 13 months, losing by one miserable vote. My personal view was that the Congress should have let the Vajpayee government continue, and not vote it out, until it collapsed, as it was bound to do.

In his 13-month stint, Vajpayeeji had burnished his image by Pokhran II and standing up to US sanctions. The one-vote loss brought him a flood of sympathy. That was sufficient to boost the BJP's tally in the 1999 election to 182 and put Vajpayeeji back in the seat of Prime Minister.

All Friends, None Enemy

As far as Vajpayeeji was concerned, that was his finest hour. Not for himself but for his party, he softened the rough edges of the BJP, made friends, attracted allies, mediated quarrels, preached *raj dharma*, ceded authority to his colleagues, delivered modest economic growth and, surprisingly, dropped hints of retirement in 'two to four years' (December 2002).

Throughout the six-year period, he won numerous friends but made no enemies. That was Vajpayeeji's distinguishing hallmark. When he left office in May 2004, and when he died last week, everyone had nothing but good and kind words to say about him.

I wish to recall two events that involved Vajpayeeji and me.

The first was in 1988–1989. The Bofors case had hobbled the Rajiv Gandhi government. The brief was handled in Parliament by a succession of ministers until it landed in my lap in late 1988. After studying the record carefully, I came to the conclusion that money had indeed been paid by AB Bofors to secure the contract, but there was no evidence that an Indian minister or an Indian official had received the money. I sought and obtained Rajiv Gandhi's permission to make this important statement at the next available opportunity. The opportunity came within days. Vajpayeeji opened one more debate on Bofors. Answering on behalf of the government, I made my statement based on my conclusion. I still remember the look of puzzlement on Vajpayeeji's face. He rose to admonish me and said that he 'did not expect Mr Chidambaram to make a statement exonerating the bribe takers', or words to that effect. I insisted that I was speaking the truth. (On 4 February 2004, a judge of the Delhi High Court threw out the CBI's charges against Rajiv Gandhi.)

A Man of Grace

The second was in 1997–1998. I was finance minister in the United Front government and was piloting the Bill to throw open insurance to the private sector, including foreign investors. The main opposition came from the BJP and the main grievance was the clause permitting foreign investment. To find agreement, I offered to limit the foreign holding to 20 per cent. Vajpayeeji agreed. The stumbling block was Mr Murli Manohar Joshi, but Vajpayeeji promised me that his party would support the Bill. After the debate was over, voting started, clauses 2 to 12 were passed, but Mr Joshi opposed clause 13 that allowed FDI. Vajpayeeji took me behind the Speaker's chair and expressed regret for being unable to keep his promise. The Bill faced defeat, but I refused to withdraw it. I.K. Gujral, Prime Minister, stepped in and the Bill was withdrawn. (Poetic justice was a few months away. In 1999, the Vajpayee government passed the same Bill with substantially the same clause on FDI.)

I was not a Member of Parliament during 1999–2004. I turned columnist and did not spare the Vajpayee government. Not once did I get the sense that someone in the Vajpayee government was watching and counting the brickbats.

Vajpayeeji was a true democrat who recognised the legitimate role of the Opposition. History will remember him as a good and kind man, a gentle colossus.

WILL CONSTITUTIONAL VALUES SURVIVE ELECTIONS?

9 December 2018

You will read this essay two days after the last of the five states have voted (7 December) and two days before counting (11 December). I can, therefore, afford to be less circumspect!

The five states that went to polls are not exactly representative of the whole country. Madhya Pradesh, Chhattisgarh and Rajasthan are among the poorer states of India, culturally rich, socially conservative/regressive, educationally backward and economically on the lower rungs of the ladder. Mizoram is high on human development but resource-poor and hence a relatively poor state. Telangana is a state that can be whatever it wants to be but it still looks like a start-up and not a grown-up.

The results of the elections will be conclusive for the people of the five states but will be inconclusive for the rest of the country. Unless Mizoram and Chhattisgarh produce 'hung' Assemblies, it is possible that in all the five states a government with a clear majority will be formed. That will signal to the world that despite attempts to erode institutions and liberty, democracy is thriving in India, though slightly bruised.

Factors Common and Different

There were factors common to the five states: Mr Narendra Modi, the tireless campaigner; Mr Rahul Gandhi, the feisty challenger;

soaring unemployment; farmers' distress, debt and agony; rampant use of money; unconcealed attempts to polarize the electorate; and questions about Electronic Voting Machines (EVMs).

There were key differences too. In Madhya Pradesh and Chhattisgarh, the BJP chief ministers were undefeated veterans of three successive terms aiming for a historic fourth term. In Rajasthan, the BJP chief minister had alternately won and lost, and this time it was her turn to lose! In Mizoram, the Congress chief minister had a record of service and sacrifice (in favour of Laldenga), but this time he was challenged by his erstwhile colleagues. In Telangana, the youngest state in the Union, the runaway victor of 2014 was fighting to save his government and his pride.

The results of the elections will be important for the country and for the two major parties, the BJP and the Congress. The aftermath of the results will be more important—how many of the constitutional values survived the bitterly fought elections. I think we should ask ourselves, of what purpose are elections if after every election a bit of the Constitution perished?

Values at Stake

So, let me count the constitutional values that are at stake.

At the top is the value of free and fair elections that is entrusted to the care of the EC. The EC has failed the people in many ways, the gravest failure being its inability to curb the use of unaccounted money. Expenditure limits are a farce. People are inclined to think that elections can be fought only by candidates who are rich or corrupt or both. If the candidates do not have money, the party must have hoards of cash to fund its candidates—like Jayalalithaa did—and the BJP is widely believed to be doing now. The EC has also failed the people by its unwillingness to improve the security of the EVM-VVPAT system of polling and counting. The minimum it could do is to match the EVM count with the VVPAT count in at least 25 per cent of the polling units. It will mean a delay of about two-three hours in declaring the result, but that is a very small price to pay to win the confidence of the people.

Next is the value of a free media. Some TV channels are not only pay channels, they are also paid channels. The rest, though not paid for, appear to have partially keeled over out of fear. Most newspapers struggle to remain independent, dipping their standard only when reporting the prime minister. The Congress and Mr Rahul Gandhi remain the favourite punching bags, but the punches are landing more softly as the Congress's graph rises more visibly. Before the Lok Sabha elections, the media must find a way to reclaim its position as the fearless and independent fourth estate.

Third, is the value of a free vote. With every election, the caste calculus is becoming the most important criterion—from selection of candidates to formation of governments. Every rise in the importance of caste means that the importance of other factors—party-narrative, leadership, performance, candidate-merit, manifesto promises, etc—is diminishing rapidly.

Fourth, is the value of a constituency's verdict. If the victor betrays the verdict and behaves like a trapeze artist—swinging from one party to another—of what purpose is the candidate-based, constituency-specific election? We may have to seriously consider alternatives.

Notwithstanding the above, the results will be declared on 11 December. Here are some whispers in the corridors:

- Friends in the Congress and the BJP say that the Congress will win Rajasthan!
- Friends in the Congress say that the Congress will win Madhya Pradesh, friends in the BJP are silent!
- In Chhattisgarh, the Congress may fall just short of a majority. In a hung Assembly, no one knows what BSP-Jogi will do!
- A person close to the chief minister of Telangana has confidentially called the state for the Congress!
- No one is able to predict the outcome in Mizoram except to say that the BJP is waiting to play mischief!

A HUNDRED-DAY JOURNEY

16 December 2018

Congress-mukt Bharat was always a chimera. The BJP, and particularly its two leaders, Mr Narendra Modi and Mr Amit Shah, tried to sell the fatuous idea that the Congress party can and will be wiped out of the electoral map of the country. The Congress rubbished the argument. Even the RSS distanced itself from the provocative slogan. The people of India, however, seem to have taken offence to the BJP's plan.

When the opportunity arose, the electorate in the three states of Chhattisgarh, Rajasthan and Madhya Pradesh voted decisively in favour of the Congress that was locked in a direct fight with the BJP. Readers may demur at the use of the word 'decisively', but I do so deliberately and after a careful analysis of the results.

Decisive Verdict

Consider the following facts:

In Chhattisgarh, the Congress won the highest number of seats by any party (68/90) with 43.0 per cent of the votes polled, since the formation of the state.

In Rajasthan, the Congress inched ahead of the BJP both in the popular votes (13,935,201 vs 13,757,502) and percentage of votes polled (39.3 per cent vs 38.8 per cent). Besides, the Congress gave away five seats to its allies who polled 184,874 votes, which must be added to the Congress' tally.

In Madhya Pradesh, the Congress contested one seat less than the BJP, yet the Congress got more seats (114 vs 109) and polled an almost equal number of votes (15,595,153 vs 15,642,980).

Considering from where the Congress started the race in the three states, the fact that the Congress pulled level with the BJP is the decisive nature of the people's verdict. The results would have been even more decisive if the BSP had allied with the Congress. In Rajasthan, the BSP won six seats (4.0 per cent and 1,410,995 votes) and in Madhya Pradesh two seats (5.0 per cent and 1,911,642 votes). An alliance between the two parties would have added 29 seats in Madhya Pradesh to the Congress's number of 114.

Reasons behind Results

Enough of the numbers. Let's ask ourselves why the people voted so decisively in favour of the Congress. The principal causes in the Hindi heartland are well known—farmers' distress, unemployment, and insecurity among women, Dalits, tribals and minorities. Beyond the Hindi heartland too, the same factors are at play. Whether an incumbent BJP government at the Centre would be able to resist the powerful negative wave is the million dollar question in the run-up to the Lok Sabha elections in 2019.

At a deeper level, I think there are several other factors at play. Do not make the mistake of assuming that the average citizen is concerned only with the bread-and-butter issues of prices and jobs. She is concerned, certainly at the subliminal level, with other issues.

Consider, for example, the effect of Mr 'Yogi' Adityanath, the chief minister of the largest state, Uttar Pradesh. Mr Adityanath was a tireless campaigner like Mr Narendra Modi and addressed more rallies than Mr Modi did. When such a person speaks—and speaks only—of protecting the cow, building a Ram temple, erecting the tallest statue of Lord Ram, renaming cities, banishing Muslim leaders from their states, etc, he does not convey a message of hope or development or security. On the contrary, he raises the spectre of constant conflict, violence, riots, and polarization and division of society, and drives fear into the hearts of average citizens. Such fear, in my view, is a potent factor behind the voting behaviour of the very poor: they can live with poverty and betrayed promises of development, but they cannot live in a situation of perpetual conflict.

We Must Banish Fear

On the rest of the electorate too, the effect of a Mr Adityanath is nearly the same. Add to that speeches of the kind delivered in the last phase of the elections by Mr Modi and Mr Shah, and the picture is complete and terrifying. If you think that fear does not affect the voting behaviour of the senior citizen or the homemaker or the ambitious professional or the aspiring young student, you are wrong. In the last week, a number of usually discreet business persons and bankers have warmly shaken my hand and whispered their congratulations to the Congress party! An educated young lady, pushing her trolley, raced to catch up with me to say how happy she was with the election results and to wish the Congress the best of luck. Senior citizens at lunch stopped me to say they were thrilled by the results and hoped there would be change in 2019. Journalists, the most hardened and cynical among the observers of the political situation, have sought interviews (although I do not yet know what their proprietors think!).

Make no mistake, the BJP will fight back with all the instruments in its hands—laws, ordinances, promises, searches, prosecutions and above all with more money thrown into ongoing programmes. As for more money, the chances of the government raiding the so-called 'excess reserves' of the RBI have improved with the exit of Dr Urjit Patel.

The BJP has a hundred days to fight back. The Opposition also has a hundred days to take the battle forward. The verdict of 2019 will decide the fate of the Constitution of India and its values.

JAMMU AND KASHMIR

Ignoring warnings from many quarters, including retired Army generals, the central government continued with its thoroughly misconceived muscular, militaristic policy in J&K. The opportunistic alliance of the PDP and BJP collapsed and the state was brought under Governor's Rule. It was no better as the governor made numerous mistakes. I am afraid that the BJP and the central government are walking on a road to disaster in J&K.

REVISITING JAMMU AND KASHMIR

7 January 2018

From time to time we are rudely reminded that there is an issue concerning the state of J&K. The last reminder came on the night of 30–31 December 2017, when militants attacked the Central Reserve Police Force (CRPF) Training Centre at Lethpora in Pulwama district killing five CRPF personnel and injuring three.

Different sections of the people—and of the polity—have different views on the issue of J&K. At one extreme is the position of the Hurriyat: secession. They know their goal of seceding from the Indian Union is impossible and can never be achieved. At the other extreme is the hard, muscular, militaristic position of the BJP. They know that will never lead to a political solution.

We cannot allow ourselves to be caught between a hard place and a hard place. If we do, the losers will be the people of J&K and India will lose the opportunity to find a political solution. Fortunately, that need not be so, and there are many initiatives that can be taken that will pave the way to a political solution of the Kashmir issue.

I have written extensively on J&K. Please read the five essays that appeared between 17 April and 18 September 2016, and the two essays that appeared on 16 April 2017 and 16 July 2017 (in *The Indian Express*).

A Pre-election Gimmick

On the eve of the election in Gujarat, the government appointed

Mr Dineshwar Sharma as Special Representative (SR), but his mandate was not clear. Subsequently, it was indicated that the SR will talk to anyone who was willing to meet him, and therein lies the catch.

The government—and the BJP—had branded the Hurriyat as secessionists and asserted that there will be no talks with them, ever.

The government—and the BJP—had branded the demand for *azadi* as no different from the demand for secession and asserted that there will be no talks with those who demand *azadi*.

Year	Civilian	Terrorists/Militants	Security Forces
2014	28	110	47
2015	17	108	39
2016	15	150	82
2017*	40	206	75
2017**	57	218	83

*up to 14 December, MHA
**Institute for Conflict Management

Infiltration and militancy, supported by Pakistan, have caused turmoil in J&K (see Table). But it would be wrong to think that the issue is infiltration and militancy. Infiltration and militancy are the consequences of the issue. The issue is the long-pending dispute concerning the accession of Kashmir. The state of J&K was forcibly divided following the first war between India and Pakistan in 1947, and remains divided until this day. Four wars have been fought over the issue. No purpose will be served by pretending that there is no issue or there is no dispute between India and Pakistan.

Vajpayee vs Narendra Modi

Wisdom lies in actively working to find a political solution to the issue of J&K. Both Mr A.B. Vajpayee and Dr Manmohan Singh will be remembered for their diligent efforts to find a solution to the issue. On several occasions, a solution seemed to be within our grasp, but the solution—if there was one—slipped out of our hands. The fault of the present government is that it does not seem to want a solution; it is not making a diligent effort to seek a solution; and by shutting the door on talks with all the stakeholders, it has foreclosed a solution in the near future.

The way forward is to invite all stakeholders for talks. Unfortunately, the stakeholders have perceived the appointment of the SR as a pre-election gimmick and have totally rebuffed the good fellow. Without diminishing the importance of those who met him (from a fruit growers' association to a football association), take a look at the list of stakeholders who did *not* meet him: political parties such as Congress, National Conference and CPI(M); Hurriyat Conference; recognized Students Unions; Trade Unions; politically active youth groups.

The policy of 'no talks' with the Hurriyat or those who demand *azadi* or those who were arrested for stone pelting (all citizens of India) had doomed the mission to failure.

Try Alternative Approach

Still, all is not lost. I support the idea of interlocutors, but that step has to be part of a set of measures. Here are the measures that I had outlined in my essay of 16 April 2017:

- Promulgate Governor's Rule in the state
- Announce that the central government will hold talks with all stakeholders
- Appoint interlocutors to pave the way for talks
- Reduce the presence of the Army and para-military in the Kashmir Valley and hand over the task of maintaining law and order to the state police and
- Strengthen the defence of the border with Pakistan and take deterrent action against infiltrators and militants

I stand by every word. If you are one of those who had thought that the hard, muscular, militaristic approach of the government should be given a chance, please look at the Table once again. You may change your view.

INDIA IS FAILING THE TEST ON JAMMU AND KASHMIR

13 May 2018

Mr Ram Madhav is the pointsman of the RSS and the BJP-led central government for India's foreign relations and J&K. (Is there an irony in that?) On the government's J&K policy, he once said: 'The government will stand firm, eruption or no eruption.'

Mr Madhav is safe and secure at his residence and offices in Delhi, and I wish him well. Rajavel Thirumani, 22, was not. He is dead, killed by a stone pelted by thoroughly misguided young men. It was an unpardonable crime under any circumstances. Thirumani's mistake was that he and his family had joined a group of employees, availing of their leave travel concessions, to visit Kashmir as tourists.

There was no animosity between the stone-pelting youth of Kashmir Valley and Thirumani's family. His death was, what is heartlessly called, collateral damage. Unfortunately, the death of the young man was—and is—not the only collateral damage of the 'stand firm' policy of the BJP-led central government. Much more has been damaged in the last three years.

Pillars in Danger

Among the pillars (that hold India together) that have been damaged are:

1. *A Constitutional provision will be honoured.* Article 370 was a

historical compact between the Union of India and the Ruler of the princely state of J&K. It is not the only special provision concerning a state. There are other provisions such as Article 371 to Article 371(I). Another special provision will be added after the negotiations that are underway between the central government and NSCN (I-M) are concluded and an agreement is reached. Is it the intention to breach that agreement or ask for the repeal of the new Article thirty or forty years hence?

2. *The Armed Forces will be apolitical.* On the day all the political parties in J&K resolved unanimously to call upon the central government to announce a unilateral ceasefire, the Army Chief defined *azadi* (according to his perception) and warned, '*Azadi* is not going to happen, never... If you want to fight us, then we will fight you with all our force.' Was that the central government's official answer to the demand for a unilateral ceasefire?

3. *The Council of Ministers will be collectively responsible to the legislature and the people.* There is a Council of Ministers in J&K. It is hopelessly divided: one half acts as if it were the government of Jammu and the other half acts as if it were the government of Kashmir. Even as the chief minister demanded a unilateral ceasefire from Ramzan till Eid, the deputy chief minister said, 'A ceasefire cannot be implemented from only one side.'

Insincere Actions

4. *Every executive action will be responsible action.* In J&K, this principle stands on its head: every executive action is an impulsive and insincere action. From inviting the prime minister of Pakistan to the swearing-in of the new government in May 2014 to the impromptu visit of Mr Narendra Modi to the nuptials of Prime Minister Nawaz Sharif's granddaughter in December 2015 to the despatch of an all-party delegation to J&K in September 2016 to the triumphal announcement of a cross-border action (the so-called 'surgical strike') by the Army in end-September 2016 to the appointment of an interlocutor in October 2017, there was

not one decision that was part of a well-thought-out policy. No one in the Kashmir Valley believes in the sincerity of the central government. That explains why the all-party delegation was firmly rebuffed and why the interlocutor is no longer seen or heard.

5. *The integrity of J&K will be preserved.* Many people no longer believe that J&K will remain a composite state, some even mistakenly believe that the three regions should go their separate ways. The Jammu region is polarized as never before and there are more incidents on the Jammu border (with Pakistan) than on the Kashmir border. The Ladakh region has distanced itself from the Kashmir Valley, but that region too is divided between pre-dominantly Buddhist Ladakh and pre-dominantly Muslim Kargil. The Kashmir Valley is simmering to a boiling point. A muddle-headed policy has deepened the alienation between the three regions.

Rising Violence

6. *The king will never raise the sword against his own people.* With great sorrow, it must be admitted that there is an undeclared internal war in the Kashmir Valley. The muscular, militaristic approach to quell dissent (including stone-pelting) has pushed the Valley to the brink of disaster. Violence and death are on the rise (see Table).

Year	Incidents*	Security Forces Killed	Civilians Killed	Terrorists Killed
2012	220	38	11	50
2013	170	53	15	67
2014	222	47	28	110
2015	208	39	17	108
2016	322	82	15	150
2017	342	80	40	213
2018 (up to 6 May 2018)**	-	28	32	72

Source: *Ministry of Home Affairs; **Institute for Conflict Management

The PDP-BJP coalition government lacks even a shred of legitimacy, yet the chief minister, Ms Mehbooba Mufti, will not end the farce that is becoming a tragedy.

As every day passes, I despair more. All that India, as a nation, has stood for—unity, integrity, pluralism, religious tolerance, a government accountable to the people, dialogue to resolve differences, etc—are on test in J&K. India, as a nation, is failing the test.

THE REMAINS OF THE DAY

24 June 2018

Only a few weeks ago I had poured out my anguish in an essay titled 'India is failing the test on J&K' (*The Indian Express*, 13 May 2018). I had no hesitation in blaming the BJP-led central government's policy for the rapidly deteriorating situation in J&K, especially in the Kashmir valley.

The bottom of the policy collapsed a few days ago. The BJP pulled out of the coalition government and the other partner, the PDP, had no choice but to resign. J&K has come under Governor's Rule, which is a euphemism for direct rule by the central government.

Not many in the rest of India seem to have comprehended the gravity of the situation. They were taken in by the pronouncements of those in authority, beginning with the prime minister. It is easy to be mesmerised by the promise that 'infiltration will be stopped, terrorism will be stamped out, secessionists will be punished, peace will return to the state, and J&K will remain an integral part of India'. Every call to pause and reflect was rebuffed; every criticism was dubbed anti-national.

Recall Their Words

Lest you forget, the pointsman of the RSS and BJP spelt out the government's policy on more than one occasion: 'The government will stand firm, eruption or no eruption.' It is that government which collapsed on 19 June 2018, without even a token apology to the people of India.

The home minister had, a few months ago, made the intriguing statement that 'a solution has been found to the J&K issue'. On 20 June 2018, after Governor's Rule was proclaimed, the minister directly in charge could only say, unconvincingly, 'The Centre will not tolerate terrorism any longer.' Not a word about the mysterious solution that his government had found!

When the political parties demanded a ceasefire for the Ramzan month, the Chief of Army Staff had taken upon himself the responsibility of answering the demand and had said, '*Azadi* is not going to happen, never… If you want to fight us, then we will fight you with all our force.' Following the imposition of Governor's Rule, he repeated the cliched phrase that 'anti-terror operations will continue' and added 'we don't have any kind of political interference'. The one person who did not speak (until Friday 6 p.m.) was the prime minister.

The Price We Paid

I take no satisfaction that numerous persons have affirmed what I had said three years ago: that the PDP-BJP coalition was an unnatural and opportunistic alliance. It was rejected on Day One by the people of the Valley. The PDP was viewed as the betrayer and the BJP as the usurper. When a by-election was held in Srinagar constituency, the turnout was 7 per cent. The coalition was the main provocation for the increase in violence. In the 48 months since 26 May 2014, there has been more infiltration, more casualties and more violence than in any comparable period in the past.

Several fundamental principles have suffered major damage. Contrary to the written and unwritten rules, Army generals made political statements, the J&K Council of Ministers broke the principle of collective responsibility, the integrity of the state (consisting of three regions) was severely impaired, and the state unleashed violence against its own people, including its young citizens. The table below captures the deterioration in the situation since the BJP formed the central government in 2014:

Year	Security Forces Killed	Civilians Killed	Terrorists Killed
2013	53	15	67
2014	47	28	110
2015	39	17	108
2016	82	15	150
2017*	83	57	218
2018* (as on 17 June)	40	38	95

*Institute for Conflict Management

Unanswered Questions

Several questions arise:

1. Will Governor's Rule mean more of the 'muscular, militaristic' approach to quell protests? Who will be the governor when Mr N.N. Vohra's term comes to an end this month? (Mr Vohra is an old and seasoned hand, but his age is a factor against his continuance. The true intentions of the BJP will be revealed when a new governor is appointed.)
2. Will it be a one-point agenda under Governor's Rule: use massive force to stamp out terrorism? No one supports terrorism, but one cannot be blind to the fact that it is the unresolved political question that has motivated many young men to take to violence.
3. Will the government talk to the stakeholders? The present government utterly lacks credibility. Even if talks were offered, no one will talk to the government's representatives. However good and well-meaning Mr Dineshwar Sharma may be, his usefulness is over. It is time for independent interlocutors drawn from civil society to attempt to re-engage with the people of J&K, but that seems impossible under the present dispensation.

4. Will there be fresh elections to the state legislature? There is the danger of a massive boycott of elections, at least in the Kashmir valley.
5. Will there be a war with Pakistan? It will take only a few short steps to go from 'surgical strike' to a 'limited war'. The temptation will be high, especially in the year leading to an election.

I cling to the hope that Kashmir is not lost forever, but the situation is pretty close to that catastrophe.

IN JAMMU AND KASHMIR, THE ROAD TO DISASTER

14 October 2018

We have a new governor of J&K, a new chief secretary, a new director general of police and a new adviser on security. The best outreach to the people of J&K (especially the Kashmir Valley) that they could come up with was to hold elections to the local bodies (panchayats and municipalities) in the state. The outreach was met with a rude rebuff when, in the first and second phases of the elections, the turnout in the Kashmir Valley was 8.2 per cent and 3.3 per cent respectively. There was no candidate or there was no vote cast in many wards; in many wards, the sole candidate was 'elected' unopposed!

The country had been forewarned. The Hurriyat had called upon the people to boycott the elections; the former DGP had warned (before he was abruptly removed) that the time was not opportune to hold the elections; and two of the four major parties in the state, the National Conference and the People's Democratic Party (PDP), had decided to stay away. The third major party, the Congress, agonised over the decision but, eventually, decided to honour the wishes of the rank and file of the party. However, the Congress made it clear that if the security situation did not improve, it would review the decision. Yet the government went ahead with the elections.

The elections were held under conditions that were unheard of: no list of candidates! In the Kashmir Valley, the candidates were 'secured' by huddling them into hotels. No campaign, no publicity, no nothing, and yet it was called an election! It was a farce.

Polarization Is Complete

J&K is polarized as never before. Jammu is at odds with the Kashmir Valley, Leh leans towards Jammu and Kargil leans towards the Valley, but both Leh and Kargil also assert their identities. The situation was always complex; it has been confounded by the selfish agenda pursued by the BJP. The PDP was a collaborator until the unnatural coalition government collapsed on 19 June 2018.

J&K has, for many years, cried out for a political solution. Atal Bihari Vajpayee understood the need for a political solution and how it would necessarily require talking to all stakeholders, including the Hurriyat and Pakistan. He pulled out of his rich vocabulary the word *insaaniyat* (humanity); he rode a bus to Lahore; he invited President Musharraf to talks at Agra, but ultimately he failed because he could not prevail over the hawks in his party and in the RSS and he could not contain the security forces operating in the state.

Mr Narendra Modi's tenure has seen such wild swings in approach that one is hard put to determine if there is a policy at all. 'Blow hot, blow cold' would be a charitable description of the numerous flip-flops. The BJP, as a political party, always believed—and more so under Mr Modi—in a muscular, militaristic and maximalist policy to suppress dissent and enforce law and order. It has stoked hyper-nationalism to consolidate its position in the Jammu region. It also believes it has found another ghost to slay—the 'misguided' youth of Kashmir—and, thereby, rally the hyper-nationalist elements in the rest of the country.

Why Are People Dying?

The country has paid and is paying a heavy price for the flawed policy of the BJP-led NDA. Pakistan has not been tamed. The muscular approach has not stopped infiltration: the number of attempts by militants to infiltrate across the border has increased every year, from 121 (2015) to 371 (2016) to 406 (2017). The massing of security forces in the state could not prevent attacks at Nagrota (2016); Kulgam, Anantnag and Pulwama (2017); and Shopian (2018). The worst consequence of the policy is the increase in the number of young men joining the ranks of the militants in the state: a report in *The Hindu* (27 August 2018) said the number had increased from 126 (2017) to 131 (2018). Casualties are on the rise (see Table):

	Civilians	Security Forces	Militants/ Infiltrators
2013	20	61	100
2014	32	51	110
2015	20	41	113
2016	14	88	165
2017	57	83	218
2018 (Until September)	54	71	173

Source: South Asia Terror Portal. MHA numbers are marginally lower.

The Gains Undone

There hasn't been the promised development in the state. In some areas, the state has regressed. The drop-out rates have increased from 6.93 to 10.3 per cent for primary students and from 5.36 to 10.2 per cent for upper primary students. The doctor to population ratio has worsened from 1:1552 to 1:1880. According to CMIE, private projects valued at only ₹65 crore have been announced for the Valley in the last three years. Credit offtake has missed the target by a wide margin in 2016–17 (₹16,802 crore against ₹27,650 crore) and in 2017–18 (₹10,951 crore against ₹28,841 crore).

Nor has there been any progress in winning the peace. The interlocutor appointed in October 2017 has been totally forgotten. By pandering to its base in Jammu, including support to the suspects in the rape and murder at Kathua, the BJP has further isolated the people of the Kashmir Valley. The progress achieved between 2001 and 2014 has been undone.

If the situation looks bad today, it could be worse tomorrow.

THE SOCIAL CHALLENGE

If there is one matter on which all except the BJP are agreed it is that India, today, is more polarized and divided as never before. I wrote about children, the very poor at the bottom of the ladder, unemployment, privacy and the sense of fear among different sections of the people. I coined the phrase Republic of Impunity that I fear will replace the Republic of India and the values of liberty, equality, fraternity, tolerance, pluralism and the rule of law.

CELEBRATING GODS, NEGLECTING CHILDREN—2

21 January 2018

On 26 March 2017, I had written a column titled 'Celebrating Gods, Neglecting Children'. I had said 'Our idea of human resource development is *minus* child development, *minus* child health and *minus* child nutrition.' My focus was on the state of nutrition of children and the data was based on the National Family Health Survey 2015–16. I should have added '*minus* child education and *minus* child skilling'.

There is another acclaimed report published every year. It is the ASER. We have a new report (2017) on the status of education in rural India and it was published on 16 January 2018.

Chilling Facts

ASER 2017 recalls a chilling fact that is known to all in the field of school education: ASER studies, over the last 12 years, have 'consistently pointed out that many children in elementary school need urgent support for acquiring foundational skills like reading and basic arithmetic'. Nothing much has changed except in terms of 'numbers'. Thanks to the Right to Education Act, the proportion of out-of-school children has fallen to 3.1 per cent. Earlier, children were dropping out at Class V; now enrolment beyond Class V has improved dramatically and enrolment in Class VIII has doubled in the past decade, rising from 11 million to 22 million. However, as the numbers increased, the proportion of students with foundational skills has *declined*:

- One-fourth of students enrolled in Class VIII cannot read a Class II-level text;
- One-half of students enrolled in Class VIII cannot do simple division.

ASER 2017 shifted its focus to children in the age group 14 to 18 years in rural India. The report explains the reason: 'More and more students are completing eight years of elementary school at about age 14. Just four years later, these young people will become adults. So what do these youth do during these four years? Are we ensuring that they acquire the skills and abilities they will need to lead productive lives as adults?'

Regrettably, the answer is 'no' or, at least, 'not yet'. In 2008–09, 24 million children were enrolled in Class V, but in 2011–12 only 19 million students were enrolled in Class VIII. That was a loss of 5 million. As these students progressed to Class XII, another 7 million dropped out, and enrolment in Class XII in 2015–16 was only 12 million. On a rough calculation, therefore, nearly 1.7 million children drop out of school every year.

Among the reasons are vacant posts of teachers, teacher-absenteeism, lack of accountability in government schools, absence of regulation of private schools and low government spending on education.

14–18 Years

What do the 14–18 year olds do? Most are enrolled in schools, but a significant proportion drops out every year, the number increasing with age. At age 18, 30 per cent in that age group have dropped out. One-fourth of the respondents in that age group said they had to discontinue their studies because of financial reasons. Another 34 per cent said the reason was lack of interest and 16 per cent because they had failed.

Nearly 78 per cent of rural youth in the age group 14–18—whether enrolled as students or not—do some agricultural work for wages or on their own land. Almost none aspires to join agricultural or veterinary courses, and 'the percentage of students in agricultural or veterinary courses around India amounts to less than half a per cent of all undergraduate enrolment'.

What are we doing with our 14–18 year olds? The ASER survey has found that 'there is not much evidence that children are learning vocational skills'. It found that untrained youth are not flocking to skill development courses, nor is industry chasing the training centres.

So long as agriculture is a major source of employment for rural youth, the ASER report argues, 'agriculture could use a more educated and trained workforce considering that productivity lags far behind world's leading nations'. But there are no foundational agricultural courses on offer as alternatives to the usual bachelor's degree courses that are worth nothing.

A Failed System

Our school education system is a failure. Fifty per cent of all children have dropped out at various ages before reaching the age of 18 and acquiring what can be called a 'school education'. Many of them are with no foundational skills, barely literate or numerate, not enrolled in foundational or skill development courses, unemployable except in low-skill jobs, and fated to depend on farm employment and other casual, manual labour.

Place that alongside the state of health of our children. Among children under five years of age, one out of two is anaemic; one out of three is underweight and stunted; and one out of five is wasted. It is well-documented that the first five years will determine a child's physical and mental development during the rest of the child's life.

Having the second largest standing army in the world or possessing nuclear weapons or putting satellites in orbit will not make a country a great power—or even a great people—if our children grow up into adults who are simply not equipped to build a great economy or a great nation. Reflect on the words of Nelson Mandela: 'Education is the most powerful weapon you can use to change the world'. And India.

FOR HEALTHCARE, BUDGET GIFTS A *JUMLA*

11 February 2018

Many questions have been asked about the Union Budget for 2018-19. Let me ask a few on the central government's expenditure.

What does the government spend and on what? In 2017-18, the government estimated that it will spend ₹21,46,735 crore, but it will end up spending ₹22,17,750 crore—an increase of ₹71,015 crore. How will it get the additional money? It will get it entirely from additional borrowing (₹48,309 crore that the government will borrow directly and about ₹37,000 crore from ONGC which will borrow as a proxy of the government).

Borrow and Spend

On what head will the additional borrowing be spent? ₹1,07,371 crore will be the increase in revenue expenditure. Consequently, capital expenditure will be cut by ₹36,356 crore.

That is a double whammy. The government is borrowing heavily to spend on the revenue account and, in order to find the money needed, it is cutting back on the capital account.

Did a large share of the additional revenue expenditure go to 'Health' in 2017-18? Hardly (see Table).

	(₹crore)	
Expenditure		
Health	BE	RE
	48,878	53,198
Outlay		
National Health Mission	27,131	31,292

As can be seen, the increase in expenditure, on account of health, over the BEs was only ₹4,320 crore, a small fraction of the total additional expenditure of ₹71,015 crore and an even smaller fraction of the additional revenue expenditure of ₹1,07,371 crore.

Child Health Indicators

Let's look at one part of healthcare: the state of child health and child nutrition in the country. I have looked at the data for 2005–06 to 2015–16.

- Sex ratio at birth, that is females per 1,000 male children, has improved marginally from 914 to 919. At the current rate of improvement it may take many decades to achieve full gender parity.
- Infant mortality rate has declined from 57 to 41. The world's average is 30.5 and the world's best is 2.
- Under-five mortality rate has declined from 74 to 50. The world's average is 41 and the world's best is 2.1.
- In 2015–16, only 62 per cent of children had been fully immunized.
- Among children below the age of five years, one out of two is anaemic; one out of three is underweight and stunted; and one out of five is wasted.

Because we have neglected child nutrition and child health, the quality of our human resources is poor. From economic growth to national security to technological progress to social harmony, everything depends upon the quality of human capital. Doctors have a great responsibility to nurture our human resources, especially our children, but doctors are so few. India has one doctor for 1,681 persons (2016 data) and one government doctor for 11,528 persons, against the World Health Organization's norm of one doctor for 1,000 persons. We produce only 55,000 graduate doctors and 25,000 post-graduate doctors every year. Each doctor carries the burden of at least two doctors.

Our healthcare system is broadly divided into three categories: public/government hospitals, private for-profit hospitals and private not-for-profit hospitals. Because of lackadaisical administration, public hospitals (with notable exceptions like AIIMS-New Delhi, JIPMER-Puducherry and a few others) are seen as inefficient, turning away patients and refusing to take normal risks while treating a patient. Many taluk- and district-level hospitals have become just referral hospitals.

On the other hand, private for-profit hospitals (with notable exceptions) are seen as purely profit-driven that prescribe redundant tests, procedures and treatment and turn away poor patients.

Scheme without Money

Notwithstanding free public hospitals and availability of health insurance, nearly every patient bears, out of his/her pocket, a substantial cost of medical care. The rural population spent (2014 data), on an average, ₹5,636 on hospitalized treatment in a public hospital and ₹21,726 in a private hospital. In the case of urban population, the corresponding amounts were ₹7,670 and ₹32,375. This and other data give rise to the question whether India's healthcare system is becoming more and more unequal?

It is in this background one must critically view the National Health Protection Scheme announced with great fanfare. It is not 'the world's largest government-funded health scheme', it is the world's largest unfunded government health *jumla*. A National Health Scheme was announced in the Budget for 2016–17 to cover, through insurance, about six crore families up to ₹1,00,000. No scheme was approved or implemented, or money allocated, and it was given a quiet burial. Now, a larger scheme to cover 10 crore families up to ₹5,00,000 has been announced, but not a rupee has been provided. Insurers have hinted that the premium at 1–3 per cent will amount to ₹50,000–1,50,000 crore a year and they were not consulted before the Budget announcement. There is talk of states sharing 40 per cent of the cost, but states were not consulted before the announcement. Besides, many states have their own schemes with their own branding, and there is no reason to assume they will come on board the new scheme.

It is an insult to the people's intelligence to announce a grand scheme without forethought or preparation or money in the last year of the term of the government. Having made the announcement, the government will spend its time and energies and human resources to breathe life into a dead-on-arrival idea. Meanwhile, the neglect of the health sector will continue.

THE REPUBLIC OF IMPUNITY

22 April 2018

Nirbhaya's rape and the brutal attack on her in December 2012, and her death subsequently, shook the conscience of the nation as no similar crime in the recent past had done. It attracted a description that is not often used—bestiality. She was subjected to gang rape, brutalised, thrown out of the bus with no clothes on, and left to die. Miraculously, she lived for a few days to tell the horrific story before she died in a hospital in Singapore.

Rape is not about sex. It is difficult to imagine anyone deriving sexual pleasure by forcing himself upon a woman (who is fighting him with all her strength) or a child. Rape is about the power of the male over the female, in particular over the female body. In the case of rape of a helpless child—barely a few months or a few years old or a minor—one has to look beyond sex and power to understand the self-belief that removes all inhibitions of the criminal.

In nearly all such cases, I think the accused knew that he was committing a crime, but believed that he had power over the victim, that rape was a demonstration of that power, that the law-enforcers would not punish him, and that if they tried to punish him, he would be able to marshal the support of his kinsmen or caste-folk or the police or his party or his government. The last belief has a name—impunity. Gang rape is the ultimate act of impunity.

Unnao, Kathua Crimes

In Unnao, Uttar Pradesh, the 17-year-old victim was allegedly raped by a public person (a BJP MLA) and his accomplices in June 2017. Two months later, she wrote to the chief minister of Uttar Pradesh demanding that an FIR be registered against the MLA and his brother. In April 2018, the victim's father was allegedly threatened by the MLA to withdraw the case. The father was allegedly picked up by the police and thrashed by the brother of the MLA. The father was sent to judicial custody on 5 April and then to a government hospital. The case came to light on 8 April when the victim and members of her family attempted to immolate themselves outside the residence of the chief minister. The next day, the father died at the hospital. On 10 April the brother of the MLA was arrested. The case was handed over to the CBI on 12 April. On 13 April, the CBI arrested the MLA.

In Kathua, J&K, the victim was an 8-year-old girl from the Bakerwal tribal community. In January 2018, she was allegedly held captive in a temple for a week, sedated, gang-raped and killed, intending to terrorise the community to leave the area. The main accused was the caretaker of the temple. Others include two police officers who allegedly took ₹4 lakh and destroyed crucial evidence. The state police acted promptly and the main accused surrendered in March. The Hindu Ekta Manch (led by a BJP leader) held rallies to demand that the case be transferred to the CBI for a 'fair' investigation. Two state ministers belonging to the BJP joined a rally in March. They were forced to resign in April.

Broken Justice System

The perpetrators of the Unnao and Kathua crimes knew that the criminal justice system had broken down and what little remained could also be broken. That knowledge added to their belief in impunity.

Statements add to the belief in impunity. On the Unnao incident, a fellow MLA said, 'Maybe her father was thrashed by some people, but I refuse to believe the rape charge'. Ms Meenakshi Lekhi, MP (spokesperson, BJP), said, 'The Congress will first shout "minority,

minority", then "Dalit, Dalit", and now "women, women", and then try to somehow fix the blame of state issues on the Centre'.

Silence strengthens the belief in impunity. Despite the uproar over the death of the girl in Kathua and the Unnao incident, the prime minister did not utter a word until 13 April. There were *pro forma* statements by BJP functionaries but no expression of contriteness at all. Accusations in both incidents were debunked and deflected by the BJP—blatant politicisation—yet the BJP admonished others not to give political colour to the cases!

Impunity Is Pervasive

The growing violence against women and girl children is alarming, but the belief in impunity that seems to have infected every public functionary is of graver concern:

- Every example of an institution that was captured through partisan and pliant functionaries;
- Every instance of a political party forming the state government despite losing the election;
- Every absolutely rubbish statement made by a minister with the certitude of a scholar;
- Every flight to safety of a fraudster who had looted banks;
- Every attempt to buy opponents or muzzle dissent;
- Every case prosecuted by the CBI or the National Investigation Agency (NIA) that crumbled because multiple witnesses had turned hostile;
- Every expose of an agency bending the law to violate the liberty or privacy of a citizen;
- Every killing by the police in a fake encounter;
- Every multi-crore rupees suit for defamation and injunction against the media.

All these are steps towards enthroning impunity in the place of rule of law. Unstoppable as it may seem, the duty of this generation is to stop the drift towards the Republic of Impunity.

SECOND-CLASS CITIZENS?

3 June 2018

Archbishop Couto and Mr Julio Ribeiro IPS (Retd) took different paths in their lives. One embraced priesthood, the other became a policeman. Archbishop Couto holds an important office in the Catholic diocese of Delhi. Mr Ribeiro has long since retired but is a hero in Mumbai and among police officers. What brought the two into focus at the same time was the letter written by the Archbishop to the parish priests on 8 May 2018, and the essay written by Mr Ribeiro in a major newspaper on 28 May 2018.

Prayer, Not Insurrection

The Archbishop's letter was apolitical and an appeal for prayer for the country that was 'witnessing a turbulent political atmosphere which poses a threat to the democratic principles enshrined in our Constitution and the secular fabric of our nation'. He said '...let us begin a Prayer Campaign for our country from 13 May 2018...' He asked the priests to observe a day of fast every Friday and offer penance. It was in the best Christian tradition.

It was a call to prayer, but some wise men and women took it as a call to insurrection. Ms Shaina NC, spokesperson of the BJP, said, 'Wrong to try and instigate castes/communities. You can tell them to vote for the right candidate/party but to suggest to vote for one party and not another and term yourself as secular vs pseudo-secular is unfortunate.' Minister Giriraj Singh weighed in with his deep knowledge of physics and said, 'Every action has a reaction. I won't take a step that disrupts communal harmony. But if Church asks people to pray so that the Modi government isn't formed, the country will have to think that people from other religions will do *kirtan pooja*.' Archbishop Couto had said nothing of the kind attributed to him, yet the BJP's trolls launched a vitriolic attack through social media.

The unwarranted attack on the Archbishop moved Mr Ribeiro to write an essay for a newspaper. He did not mince words, he has never done. He called out the mischief makers, recalled their past utterances and actions, and said what many would like to say: 'The BJP government of Prime Minister Narendra Modi, as distinct from the previous BJP-led government of Atal Bihari Vajpayee, doubts and questions the patriotism of the minorities! This is totally unacceptable.' He recalled that his ancestors were Hindus who were converted 400 years ago, he acknowledged that this was a majority Hindu country, he revealed that his circle of friends and colleagues were predominantly Hindu and added, proudly, 'But I rather like the religion I was born into. It has taught me the values of truth and justice and it taught me the concept of service.' A Hindu or a Muslim could proudly say the same thing about his/her religion.

Shame on Us

Mr Ribeiro's conclusion should make us hang our heads in shame. He wrote: 'I should be prepared for second-class citizenship… What I will not accept is being accused falsely of being anti-national and pilloried on that account.'

What have we done to this country and to ourselves that more and more people—Muslims, Christians, Dalits, tribals—are beginning to think that they have become second-class citizens?

I recall my school and college days when no one noticed or cared if your desk mate or your class leader was a Muslim or a Christian. The Madras Christian College High School was established by Scottish missionaries. The legendary Kuruvilla Jacob was headmaster for

25 years. The students were predominantly Hindu, with a significant number of Christians and a sprinkling of Muslims. My class pupil leader, in all the six years, was a Muslim. I recall these facts today—we did not notice them in those days—with a sense of disbelief! Most students chose Bible classes over Moral Science classes, but there was not a single case of conversion. In college, we had foreign (mainly Irish) and Indian Jesuits as teachers. I observed and learnt from Fr Coyle how to write and speak English correctly. No one attempted to convert me or anyone else.

This country owes a lot to its Muslim, Christian, Jain, Buddhist, Sikh and Parsi citizens who have contributed greatly in many fields—industry, literature, art, music, sports, politics, etc. Close your eyes and recall the names; you will be surprised by the number and the diversity.

Genuine Fears

If the religious minorities feel deep down in their hearts that their place is that of 'second-class citizens', we are not worthy of being described as a democracy, much less a republic. Mr Ribeiro's anguished cry that 'If that happens this land of mine will be nothing less than a saffron Pakistan', is absolutely true.

Under the government of Mr Narendra Modi and his cohorts in the states, unlike the government of Mr Vajpayee, intolerance is the new normal. Abuse is the new vocabulary. Hate is the new weapon. Instilling fear is the new strategy. Polarization is the new electoral tactic.

Yet there is hope when Ms Tabassum Hasan, a Muslim, can win a by-election to the Lok Sabha from a constituency in Uttar Pradesh. As long as Archbishop Couto and Mr Julio Ribeiro can speak and write, and Ms Tabassum Hasan can get elected, democracy will be safe in India.

SU-RAJ (GOOD GOVERNANCE) AND MS SWARAJ

8 July 2018

There are two kinds of mobs—one, on the ground, and the other, in the virtual world. Both share the same characteristics. The members of the crowd take cover under anonymity. They pretend to be offended or injured. They singularly lack the courage to own their actions or words. They believe they are citizens of the Republic of Impunity.

During the last four years, mobs of both kinds have grown in number and size. In the real world, mobs have assaulted girls wearing jeans and couples in a park or bar. They lynched Mohammad Akhlaq for having meat in his home (Dadri, UP) and Pehlu Khan for carrying cattle to his dairy farm (Alwar, Rajasthan). They stripped and beat Dalit boys at Una, Gujarat. There are more examples from Assam, Jharkhand, Maharashtra, West Bengal, etc where the victims were usually Muslims or Dalits or nomads.

In recent months, mobs, egged on by rumours, have killed people suspected to be child-lifters. One of them, Sukanta Chakraborty, was a young man appointed by the authorities in Sabroom, Tripura, to quell rumour-mongering!

In the virtual world, the mob is not very different. They have a name: trolls. They are intolerant, rude, coarse, vulgar and violent. Their weapons are hate speech and fake news. They may not kill, but I suspect that many of them, if he or she was part of a violent mob in the real world, would not hesitate to do so.

Lonely Ms Swaraj

One such mob launched into Ms Sushma Swaraj, the Minister of External Affairs, recently. She has been a member of the BJP (and its predecessor, the Jan Sangh) for as long as she has been in public life. She is educated, urbane and articulate. She takes particular care to identify herself with the BJP's image of an ideal Hindu Indian woman. She has won many elections. During 2009–2014, she was the Leader of the Opposition in the Lok Sabha—a position that in a parliamentary democracy should have made her the natural choice to be prime minister if her party won the election.

The BJP won the election in 2014, but an outsider with tremendous energy and political skill had already stormed his way to become the leader of the party and, therefore, prime minister. Ms Swaraj, along with Mr L.K. Advani, had resisted the rise of Mr Narendra Modi but lost. After the election, Ms Swaraj fought a lonely battle to find an honourable place in the new government and was ultimately accommodated as minister of external affairs—but with little say in the conduct of foreign policy, which had been taken over by the Prime Minister's Office.

Swaraj Invents Role

The smart Ms Swaraj invented a role for herself—champion of the little person who was stranded in a foreign country or had been abducted/imprisoned or denied a passport/visa or required admission to an Indian university/hospital and so on. Apparently, there was a need for such a Good Samaritan and the people seemed to love her benevolence. It also helped that she scrupulously avoided confrontation with Opposition parties.

Suddenly, one routine act of kindness landed her in trouble. An inter-faith couple found it difficult to get their passports and tweeted their grievance. Ms Swaraj, or one of her staff, responded and directed the Passport Office to issue the passports. The officer who had allegedly denied the passports was transferred pending an enquiry—perhaps an over-reaction, but certainly without any malice. All hell broke loose in the Twitter world. Ms Swaraj was trolled as no BJP leader had been. It became obvious that the trolls belonged to the same army that is routinely unleashed every day against Opposition leaders. Anyone who has read Swati Chaturvedi's *I Am A Troll* knows who they are and how they are funded. Ms Swaraj's fault was that she did not take note of the troll army until they targeted her.

Shock and Silence

Ms Swaraj decided to play victim. She 'liked' some tweets, re-tweeted them, and asked for a vote on how many people supported the trolls. To her shock, I suppose, though 57 per cent sympathised with her, 43 per cent supported the trolls! The point of the story is that, during the entire unsavoury controversy, not one fellow minister or party functionary made a statement condemning the trolls! Many days later, the Home Minister revealed that he had spoken to Ms Swaraj and told her that the trolls were 'wrong' but that she should not have taken them seriously! It is obvious that trolls are the new *pracharaks*: they are mobilized to serve one or two leaders (all others are expendable), are 'followed' by senior BJP leaders, and nobody will dare to offend them.

Really, Mr Home Minister, should we not take the trolls seriously? By the same yardstick, I suppose, we should not take the moral police, the love-*jehadis*, the cow protection vigilantes and the lynch mobs seriously.

Trolls and the abuse of social media mark a new low in the breakdown of civil society, law and order, and the justice-delivery system. Action, not words, is required to put down this verbal violence, especially death or rape threats. Unfortunately, there is no action; there are not even words said promptly and sincerely, by those holding high Constitutional offices.

JOBS—THE MAKE OR BREAK ISSUE

2 September 2018

The Concise Oxford Dictionary defines 'interview' as a face-to-face conversation between a journalist and a person of public interest. Keeping that in mind, the several 'interviews' published by newspapers two weeks ago with Prime Minister Narendra Modi should be called 'intraview': the prime minister answered *in writing* pre-submitted questions. It is difficult to say if the questions were prepared first and the answers later or vice versa. The answers were good, in fact too good: good and complete sentences, good grammar, good syntax, and good reproduction of Press Information Bureau handouts.

In this essay, I wish to deal with only one set of answers. It is to a question about jobs; it is the question that I am asked every day, especially when I travel out of Delhi: Where are the jobs? I appreciate Mr Nitin Gadkari's candour. Without blinking an eye or looking over his shoulder, he said, 'There are no jobs.' He could afford to say that without fear of a reprimand.

MUDRA Loan Myth

One sentence in the answer of Mr Modi should have ended the debate. He said, '12 crore MUDRA loans have been given in last four years. Even if each loan had created one job, that means 12 crore jobs were created.' If the premise is correct, the answer is unassailable, but did each MUDRA loan create a job?

The facts relating to MUDRA loans are broadly the following: since 2015–16 and until 15 August 2018, 13,37,85,649 loans had been given by the banks. The total amount disbursed was ₹6,32,383 crore. Impressive, until you work out the average size of the loan: the average amount was ₹47,268. The prime minister claimed that each loan created one job, so 12 crore jobs (actually 13,37,85,649 jobs) were created in three years and four months! Certainly more than the promised 2 crore jobs a year!

There are too many hurdles to the conclusion. Firstly, the number of people actively seeking jobs in a year is about four crore and, if 13 crore have got jobs, unemployment in the country ought to have been wiped out under the BJP-led NDA government! Secondly, the unemployment rate should be zero. On the contrary, the CMIE reported that the rate of unemployment in 2017–18 was 4.7 per cent. Thirdly, how do we explain that a total of 4,26,53,406 persons were registered in all employment exchanges at the end of June 2018? And finally, how do we explain that the total number of employed has fallen from 40.32 crore in July 2017 to 39.75 crore in July 2018?

Jobs at ₹47,268!

The reality is that a loan of ₹47,268 is not sufficient to create a job. That amount may be enough to buy some tools or furniture or install an airconditioner or a refrigerator. It may be used as additional working capital. By no stretch of imagination will ₹47,268 create an additional job. Even if an employee is hired at less-than-minimum wage (say, ₹3,000 per month), the loan amount will not be able to generate an additional income of ₹3,000 per month to pay the wages. Mercifully, no economist has endorsed the prime minister's claim that each MUDRA loan created a job.

The truth is that jobs are not being created. There is empirical as well as anecdotal evidence in support of that conclusion. The survey done by the CMIE shows a fall in the total number of employed persons. Besides, intuitively, it is increased investment and increased credit that will create jobs, but both investment and credit are languishing. GFCF has fallen from a high of 34.3 per cent in 2011–12 to 31.3 per cent in 2013–14 to 28.5 per cent during the last three years. Besides, in 2017–18, announcement of new investment projects declined by 38.4 per cent and completion of new projects declined by 26.8 per cent compared to the previous year. Credit growth seems to have revived in recent months, but y-o-y credit growth to industry is 0.9 per cent and to MSMEs is 0.7 per cent (June 2018). Notwithstanding MUDRA loans, between March 2015 and March 2018, the outstanding loans to MSMEs declined from ₹5,04,564 crore to ₹4,76,679 crore.

Depressing Evidence

Anecdotal evidence is more depressing. I have asked my audience at several places if anyone among them had *added* one employee to his or her rolls. Not one hand went up at Thoothukudi or Thane or Kolhapur or Nashik. Ten days ago, the managing director of a construction company (turnover ₹2,000 crore) employing designers, architects and engineers told me that, far from adding to employment, he had retrenched over a hundred employees in the last two years. The government asked the Labour Bureau to discontinue its quarterly report of the number of jobs created in the economy (why?) and, instead, relied on enrolment data under EPF, ESIC or New Pension Scheme. Several economists and statisticians have torn apart those fluctuating numbers.

The proof of the pudding is the mood of the nation. Every survey has revealed that the topmost concern of the people is 'jobs'. They are not dazzled by the GDP growth number and they seem to know, unlike the prime minister, that there can be normal growth without creating employment. Jobless growth is a ticking time bomb.

GOOD AADHAAR, BAD AADHAAR

30 September 2018

Aadhaar was intended to be a unique identification number, so unique that it will not—and cannot—be fabricated, duplicated or misused. Welfare States hand out money, either in the form of cash or benefits. Well-known examples are scholarships, old age and disabled persons' pensions, subsidy for the LPG cylinder, etc. We found that a private college had 'ghost' students on its rolls and claimed scholarships for them. We found that many households had two or more LPG cylinder connections and claimed the subsidy on all cylinders with the connivance of the dealers. We found that LPG dealers had enrolled 'ghost' customers, claimed the subsidy, and sold the cylinders to hotels, restaurants and marriage halls.

The other problem was that the poor did not have a reliable method to identify themselves. The worst sufferers were migrant workers, slum dwellers, forest dwellers and people forced to live on the streets. They had no verifiable address, their names were not on the electoral rolls or any other government record, they could not get a ration card or admit their children to a school, and they were at the mercy of the police, municipal and forest officials who treated them roughly as vagabonds and encroachers.

Identity sans Identification

Not that the poor did not have an identity. They did—every human being has an identity—but they could not identify themselves, mainly because of their poverty.

The UPA government recognised the problem and its magnitude. We needed an instrument that would help every individual—if the need arose—to identify herself. And that identification should be acceptable to the provider of the subsidy, benefit or service. Hence the need for an 'Identification Authority'.

Thus was born the idea of Aadhaar and the Unique Identification Authority of India (UIDAI). Aadhaar was intended to be a benign instrument to help people access subsidies, benefits and services. Any person could obtain an Aadhaar easily and voluntarily. Any person could refuse to obtain an Aadhaar. Enrolment commenced in 2010.

Delivery under the Aadhaar project began in January 2013. It was called the DBT Scheme. The roll-out was slow and on an experimental basis in a few districts and for a few benefits. Scholarships, welfare payments, LPG subsidies, etc were first brought under DBT. The recipient had to possess an Aadhaar.

Project Surveillance State

A new government took office in May 2014. While in the Opposition, the BJP had stoutly opposed the Aadhaar project. Initially, the BJP-led government was lukewarm to DBT but, as it confessed later, Mr Nandan Nilekani 'convinced' the government. I suspect that the government was not persuaded by the technologist Mr Nilekani but by someone else who shrewdly realised the potential of the Aadhaar project to set up a surveillance State.

The NDA tried to sell the false notion that if a person could not identify himself the person would not have an identity. While more subsidies, benefits and services were brought under the project, 'function creep' also began. Ministries and Departments were directed to insist on Aadhaar. Aadhaar was mandatorily linked to a number of aspects of daily life. All opposition was brushed aside. By the time the issue reached the Supreme Court, Aadhaar was practically mandatory for the following: bank accounts, mobile telephones, pensions, school admissions, examinations, mutual fund investments, insurance policies, credit cards, post office schemes, PPF schemes, Kisan Vikas Patra accounts, midday meal scheme, Integrated Child Development Services (ICDS), etc.

The Supreme Court called a temporary halt, but the government defied the interim orders. Before the Court, the government justified the wide sweep and the mandatory linkage. It relied upon the law that was passed, fraudulently, as a Money Bill.

Ultimately, the government's Project Surveillance State has been struck down. Under the Supreme Court's majority judgment (4:1), the Aadhaar project has been severely circumscribed to 'subsidies, benefits and services paid for out of the Consolidated Fund of India'. All other areas have been prohibited; 'function creep' has been stopped. For example, Aadhaar cannot be insisted upon for school admissions or bank accounts or mobile telephones or examinations.

Brooding Spirit of Law

On the passage of the law as a Money Bill, the majority, in my view, showed extraordinary judicial forbearance. By reading down one provision and striking down two, the passage of the law as a Money Bill has been upheld. There is a fundamental error in the majority judgment, but that issue has to be reserved for another day and another case.

While the majority judgment is the product of plodding workmanship, the dissenting judgment of Mr Justice Chandrachud will rank among the celebrated dissents of the Court. It is, to borrow the words of Justice Hughes, 'an appeal to the brooding spirit of the law, to the intelligence of a future day.' The dissent sets the direction of the Court in the future and holds out hope for those who argued that the current design of Aadhaar was unconstitutional.

Every judgment of the Constitution Benches of the Supreme Court delivered in 2018 has chipped away at tyranny, enlarged the freedom of the people and advanced the cause of Constitutional morality. Project Aadhaar as envisaged by the UPA has been retrieved. The 'good' in Aadhaar has been saved. Most of the 'bad' in Aadhaar has been identified and consigned to the flames; but there is more. Eternal vigilance is the price of liberty.

WE HAVE FAILED OUR CHILDREN

21 October 2018

One of six persons living in this world lives in India. Is life in India good or bad? According to some surveys, most people living in India report that they are happy. The sense of contentment is despite the fact that jobs are scarce, the air is polluted, the water is unfit for drinking, the roads (except select national highways) are terrible, the law and order situation is alarming, and mob violence and mob justice seem to be the new normal.

While these issues are visible and are matters of concern, there are a couple of issues that are not so visible but should be of greater concern. Both relate to our children—approximately 49 crore children born and living in India who can claim a birth year in the 21st century.

Education and Health

What are a child's rights? Apart from a home, caring parents, security and friends, a child has rights that must be guaranteed by the State. These include complete education and full health.

The World Bank publishes the World Development Report every year. The Human Capital Index (HCI) is part of the annual report. The 2019 report has constructed the HCI for 157 countries. It is a measure of 'the amount of human capital that a child born today can expect to attain by age 18'. The explanatory note reads: 'The index is measured in terms of the productivity of the next generation of workers relative to the benchmark of complete education and full health. An economy in which a child born today can expect to achieve complete education and full health will score a value of 1 on the index.'

No country has scored 1 because there will always be benchmarks of education and health that countries aim to achieve. Singapore occupies the first rank with an HCI of 0.88. The first 10 countries score over 0.80. They are Singapore, Republic of Korea, Japan, Hong Kong, Finland, Ireland, Australia, Sweden, the Netherlands and Canada. Asians can be proud that the first four places are occupied by Asian countries.

The ranks of the Big Five are good but not great: the United Kingdom (HCI 0.78) is at 15, France (0.76) at 22, the United States (0.76) at 24, Russia (0.73) at 34 and China (0.67) at 46. Ninety-six out of the 157 countries have an HCI score of over 0.51, which is a measure of the progress made by humankind as a whole.

Head Buried in Sand

Among the remaining 61 countries that have an HCI of 0.50 or lower is India. India's HCI is 0.44 and rank is 115. That places India in the bottom third of the world. The NDA government dismissed the report with a haughty statement: 'The Government of India has decided to ignore the HCI and will continue to undertake its pathbreaking programme for human capital development aiming to rapidly transform quality and ease of life for all children.'

If the HCI report made me sad, the government's statement made me angry. Nobody has accused the NDA government of being solely responsible for the low HCI. All governments since Independence bear responsibility. What upset me is the unwillingness to admit to the shortcomings.

The HCI is not a number plucked out of the air. It is based on six factors, each getting a score. In the case of India, given the average household income, the probability of a child surviving to the age of 5 is satisfactory at 0.96. The adult survival rate is reasonable at 0.83. What pulls India down are the 'Learning adjusted years of school' and

'Fraction of children under 5 not stunted'. The score on the former is 5.8 years at school. On the latter, it is 0.62, meaning that 38 per cent of children under 5 years of age have a low height-for-age.

The reasons are not far to seek. While 'Right to Education' vastly expanded enrolment of children, not enough attention was paid to the quality of the schools, the teachers and the instruction. Likewise, anganwadis and 'Right to Food Security' were necessary interventions, but they have failed to provide sufficient food to pregnant and lactating mothers and to children during their first five years. Poor design, faulty implementation and inadequate allocation of funds are the main reasons.

Cruel Negligence

The HCI must be read along with the Global Hunger Index (GHI) published by Deutsche Welthungerhilfe and Concern Worldwide. One out of seven children in India is undernourished; two out of five are stunted (low height-for-age); and one out of five is wasted (low weight-for-height). The cause is undernutrition. On the one hand we have mountains of wheat and paddy and, on the other, we are unable to provide enough food to each child. At the prodding of the National Advisory Council, the UPA acknowledged the need for State intervention and devised the MGNREGA and the Right to Food Security law. Both interventions have been cruelly neglected by the NDA since 2014. The result is low HCI, high GHI (score 31.1, indicating 'serious hunger') and a low rank of 139 among 189 countries in the Human Development Index.

Given these facts, the priorities of the BJP-led NDA government are astonishing and provocative—building a temple, cow protection vigilantism, anti-Romeo squads, *ghar wapsi* (re-conversion), uniform civil code, erecting statues, renaming cities, etc. None of these will ensure complete education or full health for our children.

THOSE WHO ARE LEFT BEHIND

11 November 2018

India has the tallest statue in the world. It is 182 metres high, sculpted by an Indian and erected with the help of Chinese manufacturers and workers. Its estimated cost is ₹3,000 crore and, contrary to the myth of State funding, it was paid for, almost entirely, by central public sector enterprises.

I am happy because the statue is of Sardar Vallabhbhai Patel, a lieutenant of Mahatma Gandhi, a life-long Congressman and companion of Jawaharlal Nehru, and a fiercely patriotic, secular and conservative nationalist. As long as he lived, he did not forgive the fanatics who killed Mahatma Gandhi (as home minister he had banned the RSS for 17 months), but both the RSS and the BJP have found it expedient to forget that chapter of history.

We may take a moment to celebrate. After that moment has passed, we must turn to more mundane matters.

Chilling Facts

India occupies the 'heights' in other respects too:

- In the Global Hunger Index, India's place is 103, denoting severe hunger. Sixteen countries have higher (meaning worse) ranks.
- In the Gender Inequality Index, India's rank is 125 out of 188 countries.
- In the Index of Economic Freedom, India occupies rank 130 out of 180 countries.

- In the Human Development Index, the rank is 130 out of 189 countries. India is in the bottom third.
- In the Freedom of Press Index, the rank is 138 on a descending scale of 180 countries.
- In per capita GDP, India's rank is 140, also in the bottom third of 188 countries.
- In the Education Index, it is worse at 145 out of 191.

We can take satisfaction that India has not reached the 'height' of 182 in any index constructed after a survey of a maximum of 191 countries. However, ranks of 103, 125, 130, 138, 140 and 145 are not such that they can be dismissed in a cavalier manner by citing dubious statistics.

What do these ranks tell us? That the high rate of growth and considerable economic progress achieved by the country have not put an end to the abject poverty of a significant proportion of the population. We can debate the size of that proportion, but even at 20 per cent, it means that 250 million have been left behind. While poverty cuts across race, religion and caste, it is an undeniable fact that most of the 250 million of the very poor are Dalits, Scheduled Tribes, most backward classes, minorities and the disabled.

Inept Government

The social and political conditions have made poverty worse. We should be worried about the quality of school infrastructure, teachers and instruction. We face an acute shortage of doctors, nurses, para-medics and medical technicians. Despite liberalisation, there are still too many controls, and regulators have morphed into controllers. The heavy hand of government—through intrusive rules, high tax rates, rent seeking, and punitive powers to inspectors and investigators—has stifled enterprise. Gender inequality deprives women of opportunities and depresses economic growth. Fear rules the media world. These ills were always present but, instead of the social and political environment becoming better and freer, the last four years have seen rising intolerance, growing impunity, mob violence and the spread of hate and fear—and the government as a spectator.

The biggest disappointment has been the functioning—or the non-functioning—of Parliament and the legislatures. The Executive has treated Parliament with disdain. As a result, executive excesses as well as executive inactions abound. The Courts have stepped into the legislative-administrative void and vastly expanded the authority of the judiciary. There seems to be less faith in an open economy and well-regulated markets. In my view, the needle of liberalisation has been moved back to 3 o'clock and may well be moved back to 12 o'clock. The loser will be the economy and, ultimately, those who were left behind will remain far behind. One statistic is telling: the *average* monthly household income in the country is ₹16,480. Imagine the poverty and the hardships of families which are below or far below the average.

Lest We Forget Them

There is an old debate about who should have the first claim on the resources of the government. Claims have been made on the basis of religion or caste or gender or disability. In my view, none of them is relevant. The first claim on the resources of the government belongs to the 20 per cent of the population that has been left behind.

Poverty, as we understand it in the normal sense, is income poverty; however, that income poverty leads to other deprivations—of food, housing, water, sanitation, employment, quality education, quality healthcare, etc. Further, as long as the bottom 20 per cent of the people do not have an adequate income, they will remain victims of the hostile social and political environment. Hence, we must re-imagine governance, re-write the principles of Budget-making and replace the model and the machinery through which governments deliver on their programmes.

The 'left behind' people have become thoroughly disillusioned by the misgovernance of the last four years and are bewildered by the new promises that seem to be in the making—building grand temples, re-naming cities and rolling out more *yojanas* that are inadequately funded. The test of any promise is if it will make a difference to the lives of those who are at the bottom of the pyramid.

FOREIGN POLICY

I wrote only two columns on foreign policy and pointed out that the prime minister was a one-man band. If we count the gains and losses in our relations with other countries during the last four and a half years, it will be apparent that the gains are few and the setbacks are significant. On engagement with Pakistan, the government continued to blow hot and cold without any coherent policy.

ONE-MAN BAND CANNOT MAKE MUSIC

1 April 2018

There is a new Cold War in the world. It is not between the United States and Russia; that is a diplomatic war between a presumptuous 'sole superpower' and a chastened but proud country that has lost its pole position. It is not between the United States and China; that is a trade war that will be resolved in due course according to the rules of world trade.

The new cold war is between India and China. The war stems from two clashing points of view: India looks upon China with envy, China looks upon India with disdain. India believes China is a hegemonist, China regards India as an upstart. None of the Modi Rules of Engagement—hugplomacy, Gujarati hospitality, etc—is working.

Envy Is Meaningless

To understand the friction, one must acknowledge some hard facts.

	India	China
Population (million, 2017)	1,324	1,410
GDP per capita (USD, 2017)	1,852	8,583
Total labour force (million, 2016)	520	785
Cereals production (million tonnes)	277	580
Steel production (million tonnes)	101	831

Merchandise exports (billion USD, 2017)	303 (2017–18)	2,137
Literacy rate (per cent)	73	99
Universities in Top 100	0	6
Foreign Exchange (billion USD, 2018)	421	3,140
Army troops	1,395,100	2,183,000
Navy ships	87	317
Medals in Summer Olympics, 2016	2	70

I say it with much regret, but there can be no argument which is the stronger and more prosperous nation. It will take many years before either or both can claim to be a middle-income country that has abolished poverty. Between the two, however, China is ahead of India in that race.

China's Grand Strategy

China, by all accounts, has a grand strategy. A key aspect of China's strategy is dominance of its neighbourhood that includes large parts of Asia and some parts of Europe. China sees itself as the clear and unchallenged leader of a large and growing group of countries—in the same way as the erstwhile Soviet Union did and in the same way many European and Asian countries saw the United States before Mr Donald Trump.

India, and perhaps Japan, Australia and some south-east Asian countries, see it as hegemony; China flatly denies the insinuation. The Belt and Road Initiative (BRI) is the signature initiative of President Xi. India and a reluctant Bhutan are among the few countries that are holding out against joining the BRI.

China has entered into comprehensive economic partnerships with Bangladesh, Maldives, Myanmar, Nepal, Pakistan and Sri Lanka—countries that surround India. China's trade with and investment in these countries have increased. Bangladesh's top trading partner is China. Goods originating from China top Sri

Lanka's imports. China is making huge infrastructure investments in Pakistan, the most notable being Gwadar port. Sri Lanka has ceded 70 per cent ownership of Hambantota port that could, over time, turn into a naval base like Djibouti. In October 2016, China signed a USD 24 billion funding agreement with Myanmar and is building a deep-sea port in Kyaukpyu. The K.P. Oli government in Nepal, with a strong Marxist influence, is expected to lean in favour of China. Claiming equal rights with India vis-à-vis Maldives, China has effectively stalled any action by India in those troubled islands.

How India Failed

Observers have pointed to several strategic mistakes committed by India. The most serious mistake was the flip-flop policy towards Pakistan that is still passed off as 'foreign policy' and that has pushed Pakistan fully into the embrace of China. If there is another war, it will not be a war with one neighbouring country, it will be a war on two fronts. India's stand-off with Nepal on the new Constitution of Nepal was handled in such an abrasive manner that it hurt nationalist sentiments in Nepal and created fissures (especially with Mr K.P. Oli's party) that will take a long time to heal.

In Maldives, India has made a quiet retreat, leaving all Opposition parties in that country bewildered. In Sri Lanka, the ruling coalition of Maithripala Sirisena-Ranil Wickremasinghe feels slighted by the benign neglect; a rebounding Mahinda Rajapaksa is openly hostile.

That leaves only Bangladesh, a country divided between two political parties so hostile to each other that India will never be regarded as neutral in the bitter political fight between them.

Is there any surprise that the Indian neighbourhood is an inviting field to China that has enormous resources, no domestic opposition to its government, an omnipotent leader and a bagful of guile? (Recall also that President Xi is the only leader who has made it clear that he does not favour a hug from Prime Minister Modi.) It is obvious to most observers that China will not—as long as it can have its way—allow India to become a member of the UN Security Council or the

Nuclear Suppliers Group. China regards itself as the sole superpower in Asia and hopes to become a co-equal power with the United States (with help from a bumbling Mr Trump!).

There is a long-term strategy that India can pursue: to become an economic power equal to China. That requires collective economic wisdom, bold, structural reforms, radical policy changes and determined implementation that will lead to sustained and high (8–10 per cent) economic growth over a period of 20 years. That is a challenge beyond the one-man band called Mr Narendra Modi.

ENGAGING WITH MR IMRAN KHAN

5 August 2018

Mr Imran Khan, former captain of Pakistan's cricket team, will take guard as the next prime minister of Pakistan on 11 August 2018. His victory was not foretold, though there were strong and persistent rumours that he was the favourite candidate of the Army and therefore his win was assured. Mr Imran Khan's party, Pakistan Tehreek-e-Insaf (PTI), did not score an outright victory, but came tantalisingly close (116 seats against the simple majority mark of 137).

On the eve of the election, it was predicted that Mr Nawaz Sharif's party, PML-N, would return to power. Bets were also placed on the success of the late Benazir Bhutto's party, PPP, after her son, Mr Bilawal Bhutto Zardari, held a few rousing rallies. Eventually, the PTI emerged as the largest party.

Extreme Views Wrong

In India, there are some quarters that have great expectations from the new government. There are others who have dismissed the election as a non-event and warn the government to remain vigilant. Both are wrong.

We must understand the nature of the federal government of Pakistan. In 31 of the 71 years since independence, Pakistan has been ruled by the military. Civilian governments were short-lived and were largely at the mercy of the military establishment. The Army, the civilian government (when there is one) and the non-State players share power in Pakistan. In matters relating to India, and especially J&K, none of the three players can be ignored altogether. Nevertheless, in the jostling for power, surprises can occur and Mr Khan may be able to carve out more space for himself.

The new government will start with a certain goodwill. The government of Mr Imran Khan will talk—and has started talking—about peace, development, growth, outreach to its neighbours, international acceptance, and finding a solution to, in Mr Khan's words, the 'core issue' of Kashmir. India must seize the limited opportunity that may be available in the first six to twelve months.

India must press Pakistan on matters that the two countries can address regardless of the issue of J&K. These are the obvious ones—trade, bus and train services, cultural exchanges, access to pilgrims, tourist visas, medical visas, and resumption of sports contests. They will not lead to a solution to the long-standing dispute over J&K, but will help the people of India and Pakistan look upon each other as 'neighbours with disputes' and not demonise each other as an 'eternal enemy'. Both countries stand to reap small gains by moving towards normalising relations on a wide range of matters that any two neighbours ought to regard as routine.

Define 'Peace'

Beyond that, India does have a vital interest in stopping infiltration on the border, eliminating terrorists and finding an honourable solution to the dispute over the Kashmir Valley. There are other contentious issues concerning Siachen and Sir Creek. If 'peace' is defined as achieving closure on all these issues, I have no illusion that Mr Imran Khan and his government will play ball. So, let's keep aside unattainable goals. If we define 'peace' as ceasefire on the border, that may be achievable, as we did for a number of years. If we define 'peace' as ending infiltration, that may be mostly achievable through an agreement that will provide for joint patrolling and other border security measures to be taken by both sides. If we define 'peace' as persuading the Pakistan establishment against giving active support to terrorist groups, that may be partially achievable through patient diplomacy.

The memory of the Mumbai terror attack still haunts us. Unless the perpetrators, who have been identified and who live in Pakistan, are punished, there will be no closure to the Mumbai outrage that took 166 lives. Mr Imran Khan may—and I use the word 'may' advisedly—be interested in establishing his credentials as a democrat and as one opposed to terrorism. Nothing will be lost if we explore the possibility of nudging his government to resume the trial of Hafiz Saeed and bring all identified culprits to justice.

Mr Imran Khan has said that if India will take one step forward, he will be prepared to take two steps forward. That may simply be posturing on the eve of being sworn in as prime minister, but nothing will be lost if we take Mr Khan at his word and appeal to him to deliver on his words.

Aim for Modest Gains

Impulsive moves do not constitute policy. Flip-flop is not policy. After the Mumbai terror attack, India did not declare war on Pakistan. Nor did India declare 'no talks' with Pakistan. Those positions—unpopular in the beginning—did bring small gains. No terror incident in India between 2008 and 2014 was found to have its origin in Pakistan which, presumably, exercised some restraint. The numbers of incidents and casualties in J&K also declined dramatically between 2010 and 2014.

Mr Imran Khan takes guard on a difficult wicket. Pakistan's economy is weak and faces strong headwinds, among them being mounting external debt. The country is also somewhat isolated in the international community. Mr Khan has absolutely no experience of government. He too may want modest improvements. That's the key word: modest. Modest initiatives, modest expectations and modest results—those may yet be the result of engaging with Mr Imran Khan and his government.

EPILOGUE

I assume that you have read all the essays, or at least many of them, before you reached this page. I bet you are sad, as I am.

Miracles could have been performed with the kind of majority that the BJP got on its own (282) and with its allies (336) in the Lok Sabha elections of 2014. Indeed, Mr Narendra Modi started with a bang. If he ends his term with a whimper, he has no one to blame except himself.

In these essays, I have chronicled and critiqued the developments in 2018. Reading about these in a daily newspaper will acquaint the reader with the contours of the issue but will not give her an insight into the 'why and how' of the event. These essays were intended to convey my understanding of the 'why and how'. If my analysis has been useful to you, the purpose of my writing has been served. Otherwise too, the essays will be a source of reference to a keen observer of politics and economics. I hope you will enjoy reading them as I have done writing them.

ABBREVIATIONS

ASEAN	Association of Southeast Asian Nations
ASER	Annual Status of Education Report
BE	Budget Estimate
BJP	Bharatiya Janata Party
BSP	Bahujan Samaj Party
CAD	Current Account Deficit
CAG	Comptroller and Auditor General of India
CAR	Capital Adequacy Ratio
CBI	Central Bureau of Investigation
CEA	Chief Economic Advisor
CEC	Central Election Commission
CGA	Controller General of Accounts
CGST	Central Goods and Services Tax
CIC	Central Information Commission
CMIE	Centre for Monitoring Indian Economy
CPI	Consumer Price Index
CPI(M)	Communist Party of India (Marxist)
CRPF	Central Reserve Police Force
CRR	Cash Reserve Ratio
CSO	Central Statistics Office
DBT	Direct Benefit Transfer
DRI	Differential Rate of Interest
EASE	Enhanced Access and Service Excellence
EC	Election Commission
ECB	European Central Bank
ECF	Economic Capital Framework

EPFO	Employees' Provident Fund Organisation
ES	Economic Survey
ESIC	Employees' State Insurance Corporation
EVM	Electronic Voting Machine
FC	Finance Commission
FD	Fiscal Deficit
FIFA	Fédération Internationale de Football Association
FPI	Foreign Portfolio Investor
GCF	Gross Capital Formation
GDP	Gross Domestic Product
GFCF	Gross Fixed Capital Formation
GHI	Global Hunger Index
GPF	Government Provident Fund
GSDP	Gross State Domestic Product
GST	Goods and Services Tax
GVA	Gross Value Added
HAL	Hindustan Aeronautics Limited
HCI	Human Capital Index
HPCL	Hindustan Petroleum Corporation Limited
IAS	Indian Administrative Service
ICDS	Integrated Child Development Services
IGA	Inter-Governmental Agreement
IGST	Integrated Goods and Services Tax
IIP	Index of Industrial Production
IPS	Indian Police Service
JD(S)	Janata Dal (Secular)
LPG	Liquefied Petroleum Gas
LTCG	Long Term Capital Gains
MGNREGA	Mahatma Gandhi National Rural Employment Guarantee Act
MLA	Member of Legislative Assembly
MNF	Mizo National Front

MoF	Ministry of Finance
MoU	Memorandum of Understanding
MSMEs	Micro, Small & Medium Enterprises
MSP	Minimum Support Price
MUDRA	Micro Units Development and Refinance Agency
NATO	North Atlantic Treaty Organization
NBFC	Non-banking Financial Company
NDA	National Democratic Alliance
NHM	National Horticulture Mission
NIA	National Investigation Agency
NPA	Non-performing Assets
NPS	National Pension Scheme
NRHM	National Rural Health Mission
NSCN (I-M)	National Socialist Council of Nagaland (Isak-Muivah)
ONGC	Oil and Natural Gas Corporation
PCA	Prompt Corrective Action
PDP	People's Democratic Party
PIL	Public Interest Litigation
PMEAC	Prime Minister's Economic Advisory Council
PML-N	Pakistan Muslim League-Nawaz
PNB	Punjab National Bank
PPP	Public Private Partnership
PSB	Public Sector Bank
PTI	Pakistan Tehreek-e-Insaaf
RBI	Reserve Bank of India
RE	Revised Estimate
RKVY	Rashtriya Krishi Vikas Yojana
RSBY	Rashtriya Swasthya Bima Yojana
RSS	Rashtriya Swayamsevak Sangh
RTI	Right to Information
SAARC	South Asian Association for Regional Cooperation

SEZ	Special Economic Zone
SR	Special Representative
ToR	Terms of Reference
UIDAI	Unique Identification Authority of India
UN	United Nations
UPA	United Progressive Alliance
VAT	Value Added Tax
VVPAT	Voter Verifiable Paper Audit Trail
WTO	World Trade Organization